T0277418

THE SUN WILL RISE

THE SUN WILL RISE

A NOVEL

MISHA ZELINSKY

The Sun Will Rise

Published by Forefront Books.
Distributed by Simon & Schuster.

Library of Congress Control Number: 2023916766

Print ISBN: 978-1-63763-243-7
E-book ISBN: 978-1-63763-244-4

Cover Design by Jeff Miller, Faceout Studio
Interior Design by Mary Susan Oleson, Blu Design Concepts

For the heroes fighting for their freedom, and ours.

PART ONE

AUTUMN

CHAPTER 1

The black bag over Oksana Shevchenko's head was tight and hot.

The room where they had dumped her was completely silent. The quiet made her breathing sound much louder than it was, while the bag amplified the noise in her own ears.

Though she couldn't see, Oksana somehow knew the room was small and tight, as if she could feel the closeness of the cold brick walls on all sides. When the kidnappers had slammed the wooden door shut, the sound bounced against the exposed walls like a squash ball. It wasn't a prison cell – those were laid out differently – but it was near enough to it.

She could taste the bag's damp fabric as it moved in and out of her mouth with the rhythm of her breath. Just by feel, Oksana could tell it was made from the junk a local artisan would hawk to tourists, trying to convince them they were purchasing authentic, ancient threads. The nylon scratched at her face and chafed at the base of her neck, where the shroud had been tied shut by one of the goons. The material was nothing like the high-quality woven cloth her Baba had used when she taught her to sew coats and scarves when she was a little girl. *Typical*, Oksana thought. They weren't just bastards; they were cheap bastards.

But cheap or not, the bag had done its job. Oksana had no idea where she was.

The plastic cable ties tying her wrists felt thick and rough to the touch, while the wooden chair she sat upon felt smooth, if a little spartan. The cool air of a draft blew against the exposed skin of her forearms. Given her slender wrists and hands were already starting to redden from the pressure of the ties, the air was a welcome intruder.

Oksana was alone. She could feel it. But beyond that certainty, she could only guess where they had taken her. Hoping to sharpen her hearing and listen for clues, she closed her eyes and held her breath.

Seconds passed.

Silence. Nothing.

Defeated, she breathed in hot nylon again and again. The sound of air moving in and out of the tight fabric filled her ears more than the air filled her lungs.

Twisting her hands ever so slightly against the cables ties, the young Union Secretary thought back to the moment military police had arrested her in her office earlier that day. At least that's what they said they were, but who knew with such thugs.

Before her kidnappers' arrival, Oksana had addressed the peace rally outside her office in Union Square. Ordinarily empty and windswept, today the square was filled with life and vigour. Flags of yellow and blue flew all around her. The swelling crowd chanted messages of peace and love.

How many had been there? It was impossible to fit the whole town in the square, and yet she couldn't remember missing anyone in the sea of faces before her. Certainly, no Union meeting she had held there had ever reached that kind of capacity, and she'd seen big protests over years. The music of Oksana's country had blared over the speakers – the music of hope. It was the hope she felt the most and still remembered. Even now, in this silent room, it stayed with her. Oksana needed it. They all did.

Oksana had never felt closer to her people or to her country. She only wished it hadn't taken an invasion for them to finally feel so connected. But then, wasn't that always the case? Whoever felt this way during the good times? Everyone was too busy enjoying themselves to think at all about such things. But wasn't that the point?

And now, sitting on a wooden chair with her hands in zip ties, the crowds yelling support for Oksana, their Union, and their country were just a distant memory. But she couldn't help but think about the faces she saw earlier that day. The anxious father holding the hand of his daughter as she carelessly played in the gravel. The old ladies bravely waving flags for the first time in their lives. The young men and women with steel in their eyes. Their hearts all full of love. And hope.

Oksana had told them to maintain their faith, to never give up on their country or one another. She promised a better day would come and that, with virtue and history on their side, salvation would come. The people gave Oksana strength as she walked the gangway. And they gave her strength now.

But what had become of them? What would become of them all?

She felt a sense of panicked dread rise inside of her as she thought of the untold horrors these unarmed protestors faced in the coming days against the merciless might of those heading their way. She knew full well the reputation of those invading. They were capable of any sort of madness. They were already performing it.

Though she had told her comrades to stay and resist, Oksana prayed they had gotten away. She imagined them doing so. Streaming out of the city, their cars neatly packed with books, babies, borsch and babas. It was a nice thought, if utterly fanciful. She knew full well the city was surrounded, but the idea of a miraculous escape by everyone she knew was somehow easier to contemplate than the horror of reality. Inside the darkness of the bag, Oksana closed her eyes and swallowed.

The War had come, although no one believed it would. Even with a decade of ongoing frontier fighting, the idea of war on the scale her grandmother had described decades ago seemed impossible to Oksana. And yet the things she'd read in books, the stories that washed over her at school and at family gatherings came anyway. A sepia history had returned from the grave.

She was hardly alone in her disbelief. Signs that seemed so obvious looking back were ignored. A wilful, hopeful blindness had taken hold amongst the population as the tensions built. And when the horrible reality finally erupted, it was too late to change course.

Despite the furious fighting across the south, north and east of the country over the last four days, Heryvin – the town Oksana had grown up in, on the southern stretches of the Dark Sea – remained peaceful and untouched. Like the tensions before it, the invasion seemed almost fictious for those living there.

The explosions, destruction and death seen in almost every region had not come to their doorsteps. Yet. But Oksana had heard the stories. Everyone understood the reality. Like all her friends, she had been glued to her phone since the outbreak of hostilities, watching the outrages unfold in real time. It was an addictive nightmare.

At the rally – held four days after the Invaders had crossed the eastern, northern and southern borders into their country

– anxiety was in the air. Online news and social media sources were clear: the Invaders had broken through defensive positions and were on the march. Instagram, Twitter, Telegram, Viber – all had messages of impending doom and photos of advancing enemy troops and tank columns flowing West. Oksana recognised the images of nearby roads and villages already captured.

In the chaos, it was impossible to know how precisely far away the enemy was. But the silence was telling. The guns firing both ways had fallen quiet. The Invaders were proceeding unimpeded through the industrial areas of smokestacks, mines and large factories. Soon they would be in the city centre.

* * *

Sitting stiffly in the chair her kidnappers had strapped her into who knows how long ago, Oksana's mind wandered to her last visual memory.

She had been sitting in the Union office when they came for her. As the elected Union Secretary, she was the full-time head of the Union representing hundreds of thousands of blue-collar workers in the city and the surrounding region. Oksana was neither the first Shevchenko to lead the Union, nor the first to have the job before the age of thirty.

In what was effectively a CEO role, she was responsible for executive decision making across the entire Union. A typical day might involve managing the finances, directing

Union organisers and employees, holding one-on-one negotiations with heads of business or government, as well as dealing with major Union strikes, campaigns or undertaking worksite safety initiatives.

Central to Oksana's duties was the oversight of the Heryvin nuclear power plant, a massive industrial facility containing thousands of highly skilled Union members. One of the largest of its kind in the world, the plant was responsible for powering the region's industrial economy, as well as generating national wealth via Western energy exports.

Keeping it safe was vital for everyone.

This duty sat heavily on those who worked there. After all, you couldn't work at the plant without knowing your history. The legacy of The Accident decades before lingered in the town's memory, if no longer its soils and water supply. While those present that day had gradually retired – or worse – the lesson was passed down to those following. In Heryvin, it was an article of faith that such an incident could never happen again. No matter what.

The sheer size of the Union's membership, the centrality of heavy industry to local economy along with the enormous shadow of the nuclear plant meant the Union Secretary position had always had a particularly high profile in the sprawling city of Heryvin. But it was more than that. Heryvin was a Union town. And even in a rapidly changing world, the word *union* still meant something here.

When coupled with Oksana's position as Union Secretary, the Shevchenko family name and the city's tragic history, everyone knew or had an opinion of the young woman. It was gratifying, certainly. But walking around the city centre, a tiny old town with tight alleys, grand architecture and nosey neighbours could be suffocating.

For anyone to have what was effectively *the* job in Heryvin at such a precocious age was almost unprecedented. But for a woman to have the role at all? Well, that was utterly unprecedented. Heryvin was a city of half a million blue-collar roughnecks where disagreements were sorted out the old-fashioned way. Or, failing that, with a pool cue over the head. That it would bestow the honour of leadership on Oksana spoke to the no-nonsense egalitarianism of the place. If you were good enough, you were old enough.

But was she? Oksana wasn't convinced. After graduating university with a Master's in Nuclear Sciences, it was this lingering doubt about her own capabilities that kept her at home in the first place. While her college friends were accepting exciting offers in big cities or abroad, Oksana stayed to continue her postgraduate doctorate studies in nuclear physics. Or at least that was what she told herself. But deep down, she was connected to her town in a way she couldn't quite articulate. She didn't know why she needed to stay, only that something in her bones compelled her to. So, she did.

And when the Union leadership came knocking on the

eve of Oksana's twenty-nineth birthday, it was both a surprise and a sense of destiny that propelled her into the top job.

Though it was an honour to lead her comrades, Oksana couldn't help but feel the weight of it. She had never sought the role, and yet now here she was, acting as the town's de facto leader, central to events. In the first two years of her tenure, Oksana had performed the role with aplomb, impressing even her doubters. And now everyone was looking to her in the same way they had looked to her legendary father, decades prior, during The Accident.

Only Oksana wasn't Timofei Shevchenko, nor was substandard nuclear engineering the enemy. No pay negotiation or safety dispute could prepare her for an enemy threatening to subsume her entire life – and the lives of everyone she knew.

Maybe she should have left with her friends. She could have taken up that fellowship at Oxford, or pursued her tennis more seriously when she was something of a junior prodigy. Had she disappeared, maybe someone who knew what they were doing would have taken her place as Union Secretary.

No, Oksana wasn't her father. And because of that, she thought, they were doomed. Nobody could stop this madness. Nobody, that is, except for him.

Though much of the town's resources had been co-opted to resist the invading armies in recent days, the Union office remained off-limits due to the criticality of the nuclear safety work being overseen. If something went wrong there, the argument went, there would be no town left to defend. That's what made the events of that morning even more shocking. The Invaders knew the history as well as she did. So how *could* they?

After speaking to the crowd in Union Square, Oksana had been sitting at her simple wooden desk. A large national flag hung behind her on the wall. On the corner of the desk was an old fading photograph of Oksana taken nearly thirty years ago with her father.

The photo had been taken when he had brought her to work with him when she was a little girl, perhaps three years old. Looking at the smiling little one sitting on the shoulders of her handsome, strong father, Oksana couldn't help but feel emotional. She picked up the small black frame in her hands. She remembered this day well; how proud of her Papa little Oksana had been that day.

She remembered how important Timofei had seemed, carrying clipboards and observing the work of those at the plant. She remembered him patiently trying to explain what Papa did while Oksana giddily chased Tsar, the old brown guard hound kept onsite to presumably lick intruders to death. Looking at the beaming girl in the photo, it seemed impossible that everything in her little life would change forever less than a week later. And yet.

Setting down the picture frame, Oksana wished her father was with her now.

It was a familiar feeling Oksana had ever since The Accident. Though it took her years to truly understand what had happened, Oksana always felt a piece of her had stayed behind with her father. That girl in the photo would always be with him, lost in the haze of the past.

Whenever Oksana would have dark nights of the soul, she liked to imagine what her father would do in her shoes. Oksana imagined the answers to her many problems – an insubordinate member, a recalcitrant employer, a corrupt city official – to be written on one of the many clipboards Timofei had in his office.

Papa would know what to do, Oksana thought as she reflected on the dire situation facing her country. *He would save us.*

The picture was the only personal effect Oksana kept in the office. Everything else was business; orderly folders containing Union cards, staff files, operating procedures and legal cases were neatly stacked or filed across her desk and shelves. Her life's work, all so frivolous now.

She had swivelled her chair slightly to survey the wall behind her. Before the madness, the blue and yellow flag had felt almost quaint. It was a symbol that Oksana felt some vague attachment to, but nothing more than that. She noticed it during sporting events and – if she was travelling abroad, for example – it tended to stand out a little more than others.

But flags, borders and nation states seemed part of a

history that was increasingly irrelevant. These were the preoccupations of the world her parents grew up in, not hers. And they were certainly not the topics Oksana's friends discussed as they planned their lives in cafes, bars and restaurants – back when anything seemed possible. Now, the colours represented more than Oksana could put into words.

These were the colours flying in the cities being bombed. They were on the uniforms of those fighting and flowing in veins of her fellow citizens. They were worth dying for. They were everything.

Oksana's thoughts turned to her brother. She hadn't seen Dmytro in the four days since it all began, when he rushed to the frontline to try and prevent the inevitable. She had half-heartedly tried to stop him from going, but she knew it was pointless. Better to die on your feet and all that.

Though she hoped for the best, Oksana could read. Everywhere, experts were predicting that the Homeland would be lucky to survive a week. With nobody coming to their aid, Oksana and her people were all alone. What would come of them was anyone's guess.

With a stunned world watching, the Invaders had first crossed into Homeland territory in the early morning of a cold autumn Tuesday. Attacking via the massive land border to the East, the equally large borders of the vassal state to the north as well as the southern maritime approaches of the Dark Sea, the goal was to overwhelm with sheer weight of numbers.

And though it was early days, the strategy – such as it was – appeared to be working.

With several major cities having fallen under enemy control within days and the Capital under siege, the extremely bearish military assessments at the outset felt generous. If the Invaders had already made it all the way to Heryvin, then it seemed nothing would stop them.

With no way of knowing if he was safe, Oksana just hoped Dmytro might beat those predictions in his own small way. He had to.

Oksana and Dmytro were exceptionally close, and this was the longest period they had been out of contact. She had effectively raised him after their mother, Olya, had died when he was seven and she was fifteen. Though the medical records would show she had been taken by the town's disease, Oksana knew the real cause. Olya's body had simply caught up with her soul, which was lost along with Timofei many years prior.

In the years after, it was just the two of them. It seemed like only yesterday Oksana was packing Dmytro's lunches and sending him off to school while juggling her own studies and making sure the household was functioning. Now he was off fighting. And she was all alone.

She'd looked at the picture of her father once again and tried to remember the night of The Accident. She wished she could remember more. Like any adult, she could no longer say with confidence what was an actual memory and what she had supplemented after the fact.

She remembered Olya yelling at her to get away from the windows as she madly placed towels under the door. Sirens. The radio blaring, with a serious voice telling people to "stay indoors". A strange glow. She remembered all the women crying, how they hugged her mother most tightly. And she remembered feeling alone.

Suddenly, Oksana had been dragged back to the present as a series of loud explosions rang through the air. First at a distance. Then each one subsequently closer.

Within seconds of the first blast, a shell landed so close to the building that Oksana's office shook, knocking a stack of files from her desk and onto the floor. Seconds later, another explosion. Oksana was certain this one hit something close by. Metal creaked.

Unsteady on her feet from the staccato of the attacks, Oksana was frantic. Were these lunatics attacking the plant?

Before she had time to realise what was happening, the door to her office swung open. Oksana had counted each member of the camouflage parade as they walked in. Seven in total.

Six were carrying standard issue Kalashnikovs, newer than the ones she'd seen Dmytro and other locals carry. One soldier had his weapon slung over his shoulder, carrying a black bag in one hand and four zip ties in the other. Oksana always counted everything. She'd learned that at a very young age from her father, who had been equally meticulous in his manner. Whether it was bananas or radioactive isotopes, Timofei Shevchenko knew how many he had on hand. And so did Oksana.

Despite Oksana's protestations that she'd go quietly, the bag was placed over her head. "Orders are orders," came the stern response from the hard-faced man who'd entered her office second.

Next came the zip ties. And the smell of smoke.

Oksana was scared for herself, but also her people. This enemy was far more dangerous than anything they'd encountered before. One so reckless and insecure, it was prepared to fire heavy artillery directly at a nuclear power plant with six active reactors, just so the world would take its threat seriously.

But she tried to remain calm. She had to think clearly.

After some discussions, the men agreed to tie her hands in front, rather than behind. Small mercies for a woman, it seemed.

"For the love of God, tell them not to block the emergency fire brigades," Oksana said.

"We will," one of the men assured her.

And so, just like that, Oksana was taken.

* * *

How long had the journey in the truck been? How long had *anything* been? Days were now months, it seemed. And Oksana had barely slept since the outbreak of war.

While usually a precise measurer of time, the circumstances of her capture made it harder to assess. Oksana estimated it had been a twenty-five-minute ride, which likely putting her in the centre of the city. She thought perhaps she'd been left alone in the room for roughly twice that time.

Suddenly, she could hear noise. She stiffened slightly. Footsteps were coming down the corridor. Two feet. Then four, then six. Heavy boots. Sharp heels. *Officers*, she thought. They stopped close by.

Keys rustled. The door swung open in front of her. Cool air poured into the stuffy room, providing relief for Oksana's reddened wrists. A voice with a deep, soothing baritone broke the silence.

"A bag! No, no – this will not do," the man said with calm authority. "Cut her ties this instant."

A pair of boots advanced and brusque hands complied. With the snap of a knife, the zip ties fell to the floor.

With her hands freed, Oksana removed the bag from her head. She ran her hands through her short blonde bob, damp from the moisture of her breath stifled inside the bag. She sat with her back to the wall, gently rubbing life back into her wrists as she looked at the men who had entered the room.

Three men dressed in fatigues stood in front of her. The

flag of the Invaders was on their shoulders. Two of the three were middle-aged, one greying and lean, the other rugged and thick set underneath a cropped blonde haircut. The youngest man stood between the two older men. Carrying a brown leather business folder, he was the most relaxed of the three.

Blinking, Oksana surveyed the room. She'd been here many times before. Though she'd usually come here during negotiations on behalf of Union members or meetings with the Mayor, the City Administration building had more recently served as an informal headquarters for the local Citizen Defence Forces. A long wooden table occupied most of the small rectangular room. The walls were adorned with maps, flags from the Homeland and a single photo of her country's President.

A voice startled Oksana out of her studying. "Please forgive the rudeness of this introduction," said the younger man, taking a seat at a chair at the table. Oksana recognised the voice as the one who'd freed her. She turned to look at the man she estimated to be roughly her age. He was sharp featured, with green eyes and a sweep of dark brown hair. The other men followed his lead and sat on either side.

"I trust you understand the tongue of the Motherland?" the young man continued.

Oksana nodded.

"Good. This Native tongue of yours is . . . regrettable," he said, switching languages. "I am Lieutenant General Mikhailovich. I am head of this Liberation mission." He gestured to the grey man on his left. "This is Colonel Sokolov. And next to him is Major Golubev." Turning back to face Oksana's chair, he continued. "You are Oksana Shevchenko, yes?"

Oksana nodded.

Mikhailovich paused, thinking. "Colonel, tell me, who was responsible for Miss Shevchenko's travel?"

"Captain Grigorovich," Sokolov said nonchalantly while picking his nails. Golubev looked ahead, staring at nothing in particular.

"Summon him, please," Mikhailovich said, still looking at Oksana.

Golubev spoke into his radio to communicate the order.

Within seconds, a boyish-looking man with neatly cut blonde hair opened the door and entered. Captain Grigorovich took off his helmet and stood to attention behind the three superior officers. "Sir?" he asked.

Mikhailovich continued to look at Oksana while Sokolov rocked back in his chair to observe the young officer.

"Captain Grigorovich, can you explain why our guest was transported in such an uncomfortable manner?" asked Mikhailovich.

"Lieutenant General, our orders were clear. We were to secure the compound for mission command. All Fascists and spies are to be transported wit—" Grigorovich began.

Mikhailovich raised his hand abruptly in the air without

looking back, cutting off Grigorovich mid-sentence. "And, Captain, does this woman look like a Fascist to you?"

"She had the flag of the Fascists in her office . . . uh, af-after all, they are everywhere, sir," Grigorovich stammered.

Mikhailovich raised his hand again. "And indeed, if our guest was a Fascist spy, do you think she'd have been fooled into believing *this* building – a building she regularly visits as part of her Union duties, a building located in the very centre of her home city – was a secret headquarters she'd be incapable of returning to?" Before Grigorovich could respond, Mikhailovich looked at Oksana and spoke once again. "Are you a Fascist spy, Miss Shevchenko?" he asked.

"Is this pillow talk?" Oksana replied.

A smirk briefly flashed over Mikhailovich's face. "I see you're unmarried, so perhaps it is," he said, looking at Oksana's naked left hand. "Or are you married to the job? One of these modern women I read so much about. Is that it? No, that won't do at all. I'm afraid a marriage can only sustain one careerist, so it is not to be, I'm afraid."

"Well, I'll keep hoping and cooking," Oksana said, folding her arms.

"That will be all, Captain," Mikhailovich said, excusing the young officer as his eyes remained locked on Oksana.

Sokolov cocked his head to shoo the young man out of the room. Grigorovich saluted to his three superior offiers before hastily leaving the room. The door slammed shut behind him.

"Miss Shevchenko, I'm sure you can appreciate I am a busy man," said Mikhailovich, opening his folder. "You are the head of the Industrial Workers' Union, yes?"

Oksana nodded.

"Part of your duties involves helping to maintain operations at the city's nuclear power facility, waterworks, and dam, yes?" he continued.

"I am not directly involved in the operations. As part of my duties in representing Union members, I help ensure the safety of workers operating at the nuclear facility and, by extension, the townspeople."

"Regardless," Mikhailovich began, "I am here to inform you that your facility has been a party to a major and ongoing human rights violation against our citizens. It is my task to end this violation. And it will be your happy duty to assist me in this most urgent work."

Oksana stared at him in silence, puzzled.

"Surely you didn't believe this human rights abuse would be tolerated by the Motherland?" Mikhailovich continued. "For close to a decade, your dam and your power facility have been starving our people of fresh water in the Southern Peninsula. As you know, the Deeper River supplies close to 90 per cent of the Peninsula's fresh water. So, while I'm sure you all thought it was very clever to blockade the river," he glanced over at Oksana, whose eyes shone with approval for the manoeuvre, "which, by quirk of geography, cuts through this ghastly little town of yours, surely you didn't assume that such an act of deliberate sabotage would be allowed to stand. In fact, it is a miracle we have been as patient as we have. To deliberately deprive a downstream community of the water they need to live is a breach of international law and human rights conventions."

"Well, you would know all about those," Oksana replied.

Mikhailovich looked to his fellow soldiers before leaning ever so slightly across the table towards Oksana. "Personally, I see this as an act of war against our people," he said, his voice low, now sporting a slight edge.

Oksana's eyes narrowed. "You mean *our* people," she said, her ice-blue eyes suddenly blazing.

Mikhailovich snapped his folder shut and sat back in his chair. He glanced at the presidential poster at the end of the room. Gathering himself, Mikhailovich slowly looked back at Oksana. The smirk flashed across his face again, this time a little more contemptuous. "You seem, my dear sister, to believe there is a distinction between yours and mine. You must learn your history, Miss Shevchenko.

"There is the great Motherland – its people, its culture and its ancient history, all of which the land we stand on is part. And then, Miss Shevchenko, there are those West of here who seek to destroy it. You are fortunate, most fortunate, to be in the Motherland's very heart, to have grown in her bosom. Why, you are one of the lucky few to already be liberated from the grip of the Fascists who have swept across this land! Back into the warm embrace of the Motherland, back to safety, without a shot fired. Without a life lost. Can you imagine your good fortune!

"Soon enough," Mikhailovich continued, "this Special Operation will be completed, and the Motherland will be reunited with her people. How she has missed you all!"

He paused for a moment, allowing the words to hang in the air. Suddenly, Mikhailovich stood and began to stride around the room. "But there are always enemies within," he said, no longer addressing Oksana but instead speaking to an invisible crowd. "The Fascist Uprising in this rebellious territory has been bravely resisted for years by passionate defenders of the Motherland. It has been resisted right across this so-called country by your brothers and sisters, including," he lowered his voice, "this very town."

Mikhailovich was now face to face with the poster of the President. He glowered at the young face staring back at him, lips curved slightly upwards in a stoic, yet confident expression. "But it is time for this return of fascism to be exterminated once and for all. It is time for Liberation. Wouldn't you agree, Miss Shevchenko?"

Without an answer, he pivoted on his heels to look at Oksana once again. His eyes darted to the black bag sitting on the table in front of her hands. "And, of course, should it be necessary, there are ways to handle such Fascists – historic or otherwise."

Oksana looked at the bag before returning to

Mikhailovich's burning gaze and casting her eyes back down to the table, suddenly feeling the enormity of the situation she found herself in.

Satisfied, Mikhailovich shifted his demeanour with a grin. Returning to his seat, he reopened his folder and continued his briefing. From inside the stack of papers, he pulled out a large map. Slowly and methodically, he unfolded the large sheet and laid it on the table.

"As you would know, Miss Shevchenko, the Heryvin Canal was built by our visionary forefathers to create a large and natural flow of fresh water to the Southern Peninsula. The man-made canal allows for water from the Deeper River to be diverted from its natural Dark Sea route all the way to the Peninsula, where it is then pumped and piped for household and agricultural use.

"It is this canal that has been illegally obstructed," he continued, drawing on the map with his finger as he spoke. "In an act of pathetic petulance, this obstruction took place after the Great Reunification of the Peninsula with the Motherland. This Reunification occurred after a perfectly legal referendum process was supported by Peninsula residents, who did not wish to associate with the Fascist Uprising occurring in the Capital. But, rather than accede to the wishes of the people to rejoin the Motherland, the blockade of water was put in place by your Fascist government to punish this free and democratic independence movement.

"Now, our people – your brothers and sisters – are without water! Their very lives ruined for a decade! Unable to properly grow crops, unable to properly care for their families, their businesses destroyed. These are citizens of the Motherland, no longer able to properly manage their homes and Ordinances. Can you imagine such horrors and indignations?"

"I imagine all too well," Oksana said quietly. Though she had considered blocking the Heryvin Canal to be a tough measure, it was a fair response to the Motherland's illegal theft and Occupation of their Peninsula.

"Well, then we shall be famous friends! The two of us, restoring justice and livelihoods to those who need it. And resisting those who seek to take it away."

"And what of the safety of our brothers and sisters here?" Oksana asked. "Are you not concerned what might occur if too much water is taken away from the nuclear reactors?" Redirecting the flow of water, without taking the proper precautions first to ensure enough water was onhand for cooling, could potentially risk the safe operation of the facility.

Mikhailovich looked at her with a knowing smirk. "We have more in common than you might imagine, Miss Shevchenko. Much like yourself, I am a graduate in nuclear science – though I come from the superior schooling of the Motherland. I am well appraised of matters pertaining to the safe operation of a nuclear reactor."

"Like the dangers of firing on an active reactor with heavy artillery?"

"Oh please, Miss Shevchenko, there is no need for such drama. Leave this for the fools on social media. You and I both know that a nuclear reactor is not so easily destroyed; they are built to withstand serious shocks. A deliberate plane crash could not even hurt the hair on the head of a nuclear reactor.

"And furthermore, unlike you chaotic fools, my men knew what they were doing. My orders were clear, and the warning shots were fired shots with surgical precision.

"Provided the facility was promptly handed over – which it was, after a little encouragement – there was never any true danger of destroying the facility's cooling towers or the core itself. Even if you scare rather easily, it is pleasing to know Fascists are not entirely without rationality."

"And what of the fires this morning from your attack?" Oksana asked.

"Ha! Fires. A mere grass burn off, Miss Shevchenko. Nothing to worry about. My men had it put out in minutes. Even you wouldn't even notice the damage."

"And the spent fuel rods? As you would know, these are not nearly as secure from severe shock. They are stored in less secure, less robust facilities adjacent to the reactor and towers. It would not take much for there to be a major contamination incident. Or worse."

"Then you understand the stakes involved," Mikhailovich replied. "You needn't worry. The importance of this mission explains why I have been chosen to lead it: my training allows me to ensure there are no mishaps or lapses in judgment."

"And, I suppose, it also tells us how a man so young becomes Lieutenant General . . ." Oksana interjected.

The edges of Mikhailovich's lips curled up. "See, fast friends already," he said. "Your brothers and sisters will be safe, provided that the facility operates as usual while allowing the maximum amount of water to be directed to the Peninsula."

"Easy, then," Oksana said, looking away.

Sensing her distrust, Mikhailovich nodded slowly. "I expect, as the Union leader, you can help the workforce to remain committed and motivated to their task. There is no need for complications, Miss Shevchenko. I have a job to do. I intend to see it is done."

"In our country, it is not so simple to tell people what to do or how to work. People are free to choose."

Sokolov and Golubev exchanged a look. They knew this wouldn't sit well with their superior.

"In your *country*?" Mikhailovich said with a sneer.

Oksana nodded. "Free to choose our fate."

Mikhailovich snorted. "Surely you must know that the fate of this so-called country of yours is sealed! Our armies march from the north, east and south. Your cities and Capital are surrounded. The Fascists are fleeing into the arms of their weak, Western enablers. Our victory is inevitable, as is your loss. All that remains is which side one chooses."

"Nothing is inevitable. I believe in the glory of our Heroes. Our people will fight."

"And they will die. *That* is inevitable. I assure you that The Commander is not for turning, nor am I. Given enough time, the strong will conquer the weak, while the big will consume the small. From the top to the very pathetic bottom – this is the natural order of things."

"Only time will tell," said Oksana quietly.

"On this, we can finally agree," said Mikhailovich, his exasperation growing. "But alas, I am not here to debate military tactics or the righteousness of our cause with you. I am here to instruct you and your Union's members. You are their leader, are you not?"

"When they choose me. And if they trust me."

"Well then, you can tell them to trust you and tell them to do what we ask . . . because they simply must." Mikhailovich paused, looking at the black bag once again. "Or we can always find a more motivating leader."

Oksana swallowed slightly

"As you well know and understand, the alternative to compliance with these directives for everyone living here is most unthinkably catastrophic. I know competence doesn't run in your family, but perhaps you can succeed in protecting this town where your predecessor failed," Mikhailovich said.

Oksana bristled. "My predecessor?"

"You are Timofei Shevchenko's daughter, are you not?"

"You know I am."

"Well, then no doubt you are eager to erase the sins of the father."

Oksana's eyes narrowed. "And what sins might those be?"

"Come now, Miss Shevchenko. Your father's role in the nuclear accident here several decades ago is well documented. His disgrace and ineptitude caused the Empire enormous embarrassment internationally. It was only good fortune that prevented the damage from turning the incident into a full-blown meltdown disaster, rather than the partial reactor failure that occurred."

"My father is a hero . . ." Oksana said, trailing off.

"The official records of the Empire would beg to disagree," Mikhailovich replied.

"*Stories*, you mean."

"I will say, his ham-fisted foolishness caused a major review of the Empire's nuclear engineering program. It caused a few red faces inside the Motherland, to be sure – we are the world leaders, after all – but it did force us to redouble our efforts. The backward designs advocated by your father were replaced by the modern, six-reactor facility you have today. These are now the envy of the world! As The Commander says: you can't make an omelette without breaking a few eggs. So perhaps we should thank your father for scrambling himself and a few others."

Sensing the danger of Mikhailovich's lure, Oksana did not rise to the bait.

"In any event," he continued, "I hope for the sake of your members and neighbours you don't follow his footsteps too closely. History doesn't repeat, but unfortunately it does have a tedious tendency to rhyme. I think it was Twain who said that."

"Actually, there's no proof of that," Oksana said.

"Oh?"

"Twain, like many famous people, is often attributed quotes he didn't say."

"Well, in any event, I prefer my version. It feels right."

Before Oksana could correct him again, Mikhailovich snapped his folder shut. The briefing was over. "That will be all, Miss Shevchenko. You have much to think about and a large task ahead, no doubt. You should go home; you have a big day ahead of you. I shall see you onsite at 0600 hours."

"I'm free to leave?" Oksana asked cautiously.

"Why, we're friends and neighbours. Of course you can leave! The city is at your disposal, just as it always was," Mikhailovich said, smirking once again as he leaned back in his seat.

Oksana stood and slowly walked around the table towards the exit. Even though they were seated, she was clearly the tallest of the four. As she walked, Oksana could feel all three men looking at her. Approaching the door and close to freedom, her pace quickened ever so slightly.

As the Union leader opened the door to leave, Mikhailovich put his hand in the air.

"Oh, Miss Shevchenko, I wouldn't wander too far. It is quite dangerous outside the city limits. Especially for Fascist spies," he said without looking back at her.

CHAPTER 2

Across the country, hell falls from the skies.

Soldiers and tanks advance from the north and the east. Warships shell the southern port cities. The fighting is fierce.

City streets are clogged with panic. Pharmacies are emptied first, then the cash machines. Lines to petrol stations snake for miles. Supply lines stretch, then snap. Supermarket shelves are cleared. Nothing is left, but to die.

But the true terrors come in the still of the night. Always at night. First, the wail of sirens. Families scurry into hastily made bomb shelters. Huddling. Praying. Waiting. Then come the randomised explosions. The indiscriminate killing. "Liberation" is at hand.

The nights burn. The sun rises over a nation and people being erased. A genocide of freedom is underway.

In the morning, weary survivors survey the gaping wounds in the bodies and the scars across the landscape. Then they watch their phones. And the skies. Updating advances of armies. Searching for loved ones. Nerves frayed. They are the lucky ones.

How could this happen? Today? How?

First the targets of supposed military value were hit. Then the homes were destroyed. Then the schools. Then the hospitals. Endless Liberation. The fruits of freedom's sword.

Who will help us? Surely, they can see. Surely, they will help us. And if they don't?

West. We must get West.

Anyone that could go, went. Those who could fight, did. The women and children were first. Piling into cars, into buses. Train stations filled with desperate families. Tearful goodbyes before separation. *I will see you again, my love.*

The Western border cities swell and groan with the wave of arrivals. Millions upon millions. A sea of humanity driven by a surging black wave.

But the hell rains here too. There are no limits to the Reaper's dark reach. Not on this side of the border.

West. We must get West. Don't look back. Keep going.

Yellow school buses drive endlessly on loop. One-way commuters lucky enough to be alive. Carrying the guilt of living long enough to watch their Homeland burn.

"How long are we going for, Mamma?" says a little boy as he climbs onto a bus.

She doesn't answer. Maybe a few weeks. Maybe forever. Nobody knows. West.

A father quivers as he watches his wife and daughter take a seat in the middle of the bus. He puts a hand on the window, aching to be near them one more time. He is staying to fight. They are fleeing for their lives.

"Papa, Papa!" the little girl cries. Their hands press on two sides of the glass. The bus accelerates. Their touch slips.

Families are breaking. Worlds are upended. A people are scattered like ashes across a continent. Pouring across the border, desperate for help. Entire lives crammed into one bag. Whatever is left. *Take it.*

Crossing the border, those old enough to remember the Great Patriotic War shake their heads. Certainty has flooded the world again. Because it has been forgotten.

But the Capital still stands. Despite all predictions to the contrary, it stands. The Flag has not fallen. The Homeland, she stands.

The Flags. They fly high. They fly defiantly. They have not given in.

The sun is still rising into the sky.

The soldiers head East. The people are taking up arms.

Rides are not needed. Ammunition is required.

Surely, they can see. Surely, they will help us.

CHAPTER 3

In Heryvin, the Reaper's hand was closing slowly around a people's throat. The Motherfication had begun.

Changes were being made to accommodate the Eastern preferences of the Motherland. Liberation followed by Unification was the order of the day. Rail and road corridors that had been damaged were repaired – the ones heading east, naturally.

Nobody had seen Mayor Gerlinksi since he was marched from his office wearing a black bag in early days of the Occupation.

The Homeland flag in the town centre was replaced with that of the Motherland. Pictures of the President were removed. The Commander, the sublime ruler of the Motherland, now stared down from the city's official Administration buildings.

Merchants and shop owners were instructed to take the Mother's Oovle instead of the local currency, the Shiva. The head of Heryvin's bank was replaced with a man from the East. Though notoriously corrupt, this new manager was corrupt in the way one expected him to be. If the appropriate hands were paid, the eyes would find some place else to look.

Lusting for young minds, the Motherland decided to extend her reach into the schools. Inside the massive hall of School Number 50, Elena Kovalenko looked at the boxes in front of her. Though she was principal, with so many teachers departing westward or off fighting in the East, Elena had been forced to take a more hands-on approach to her administration.

The newly arrived boxes were stacked high in the empty gymnasium, a building that would ordinarily be teeming with young bodies up to no good. Each box had the unmistakable stamp of the Motherland's crest in the centre. Assembled in a huge wall-like edifice, the branded boxes towered over the tiny, middle-aged Elena.

It was a thankless task, but Elena enjoyed everything about her job. She loved the simple joys of teaching. It had been years since Elena had taught pupils, as the duties of school administration took the focus of her attention, but the calling never left her. With all the horrible events swirling around her, the idea of becoming more involved in the lives of children – even with a task as simple as this – was meditative. For a woman of her small stature, Elena worked with remarkable gusto. She'd tied back her mid-length brown hair and rolled up her woollen sweater to her elbows to make her job a little easier. Plus, unpacking gave her something practical to focus on beyond obsessively scrolling for the latest news from the frontline.

After her husband and son died in the Frontier Wars a decade earlier, Elena decided against having another family. At her age, there seemed little point. Over her protestations, both had signed up to defend the Homeland once The Commander had begun his proxy "separation" war in the eastern-border provinces.

The Frontier Wars commenced when the Motherland illegally annexed the Southern Peninsula. Both were a frustrated response to the Revolution of Respect – a people-led revolt that threw out the incumbent president, a politician who had been in the pocket of The Commander. He'd sought closer ties between the Homeland and the Motherland at the expense of economic and liberal freedoms, until the citizens of the Homeland decided enough was enough. Unable to generate control at the ballot box, The Commander settled on forcing "love" down the barrel of the gun.

Everyone knew those fighting on the side of the so-called "Republics" were not genuine separatists seeking independence for themselves. Instead, these ginger groups of "little green men" were hired guns, armed by The Commander himself. It was utterly transparent. But sadly, it was effective. While the Homeland fought the separatists to a stalemate and would never accede to their demands, they could not regain total control of their territory.

The conflict was particularly useful inside the Motherland, where The Commander used the perpuetual threat of external enemies and Western conspiracies to keep the people under control. Fear and resentment were powerful vices.

Despite the unfairness of it all, it seemed pointless to Elena for her boys to go fight. After all, her Homeland had never once secured its freedom from those determined to keep them in the Motherland's orbit. But both were proud men determined to fight on the side of justice.

"If we won't fight, then who will?" her son, Yuriy, had told a tearful Elena as he made his way out the door carrying his military-issued duffel bag with him.

Yuriy had died carrying his father, Vasyl, who had been shot during heavy fighting against the so-called separatists. Though she was devastated, Elena found a strange comfort knowing they had fallen together. Looking back now, she was proud they had decided to fight. She only wished more like them had.

Though she couldn't see it then, Elena now understood that bad behaviour, when ignored, only led to worse behaviour. It was as inevitable as gravity. Elena could see a direct line from the years of stupefied, collective inaction leading straight to today's unfolding disaster. *Perhaps*, Elena thought, *this madness might have ended there and then if it had been challenged more strongly.*

But no. She understood the world needed brave men and women. She only wished she could hug and kiss her sweet Yuriy and strong Vasyl one last time.

Now that they were gone, Elena's students were what mattered to her. She rode their individual successes and mistakes with the same mix of pride, stress and frustration she'd felt for her fallen Yuriy.

Opening the first box, Elena stepped back, slightly shocked. Confused, she opened another. And another. Each box was filled with books Elena recognised, only the titles were all in the language of the Motherland. She hadn't seen books like these in years. It was a jarring experience, laying bare the reality of the situation she faced: Occupation.

Though most residents had spoken both Native and Motherland – Elena herself had grown up speaking the Mother tongue – the country's official language had been Native for half a decade. And even then, Elena had only taught in the Native tongue since the Wall had come down decades ago.

Elena opened an elementary school title teaching *Azbooka*, the alphabet. *A classic*, she thought to herself as she lifted her black-rimmed glasses onto her nose, which until then had been tucked into the buttons of her blouse.

She smiled at the memories from her childhood. Her mother teaching the alphabet and language basics at the kitchen table. Long lessons at school, with Elena's kindergarten teacher patiently reading to a classroom of disinterested and disobedient children. Even after the book had imparted all of its elementary knowledge to Elena, it would follow her into the early days of her own teaching career.

It all felt like lifetime ago, because it was. Even without the War, life somehow seemed simpler then. But perhaps that was just the fog of youth.

"I trust all is well?" came a gravelly voice.

Hearing the sound of the Mother tongue startled Elena. She dropped the book back into the box before looking up to meet the voice.

Major Golubev stood in front of her, smiling apologetically. He was dressed in his standard-issue Motherland officer fatigues.

"I hope I didn't disturb you, ma'am," Golubev said, removing his hat with his right hand. In his left hand, Golubev carried an official-looking clipboard with a heavy wad of documents attached. Elena's name was in bold at the top of the visible document. "You are Elena Kovalenko, the school principal?"

"No disturbance at all," said Elena, gathering herself. "Yes, I am the principal of School 50."

"I am Sasha," Golubev said, smoothing his hat-crushed, cropped hair. He placed his hat on top of the clipboard before awkwardly reaching out to shake Elena's hand.

Elena nodded but pretended not to see Golubev's hand as she turned to open another box to her left.

Acting as though he had not noticed the slight, Golubev surveyed the room before looking at the mountain of boxes with a detached curiosity. "I have been sent by the Lieutenant General to check on the preparation for the coming school year. I trust all is well?"

"I was just reviewing the new material," Elena said, feigning comfort as best she could. Her years of teaching had taught her how to fill awkward silences with ease.

"Oh, yes, I see it has arrived," said Golubev, peering into the box. He bent down to pick up the book Elena had dropped earlier. His eyes brightened as he recognised the title. "You remember?" he asked while underlining the title with his finger and looking at Elena with a grin.

"Who could forget?" Elena said, smiling politely.

Golubev flipped open to a random page and pointed at the cartoonish drawings. "The terrors of my childhood! My Baba would bark this at me from morning to night. I see these cartoons in my dreams – no, my nightmares – to this day!" He laughed.

Elena laughed along with him with genuine humour. She knew he was right.

"But I didn't forget the lessons! Oh, no, my Baba missed her calling in life. Right now, I could quote this book word for word. I even read it to my own children. As you know, Principal, the pain must be shared across generations!"

Elena grew quiet, the moment of detached levity now

broken. She looked down at the box. Her face tightened as she looked up at the officer.

Golubev stopped laughing. He paused for a moment, pursing his lips as though he understood the torment Elena was facing. "Principal Kovalenko, it would be best to go along with the new, erm, teaching . . ."

"Regime?" Elena said, trying to finish Golubev's thought.

"Programs," he corrected, raising his brow patiently.

The silence filled the room once again. And this time, Elena let it hang there, awkwardly.

"Principal Kovalenko, these books from the Motherland are not so foreign as to be unrecognisable. Surely you would agree?" he said gently. "And as you know, these are not reasonable times. And reasonable people are all too few."

Elena nodded slowly. She did not trust him, but she understood the gravity of the point he was making.

The military officer looked into Elena's eyes, hoping she understood. "There is no value in fighting. Or having more death."

"I know."

Golubev nodded slowly, blinking. "And the children . . . well, the children need you more than ever."

Elena nodded again before looking down. Struck by the memory of the children, of her own loss, she sighed almost imperceptibly.

Sensing he'd overstayed his welcome, Golubev reached to

hand the book back to Elena. But rather than have her take it, he placed it neatly back in the box atop the others. He looked at her for a moment, placing his hat on his head. "Goodbye, Elena," he said in the Native tongue.

Elena looked at him with surprise, unsure if she'd heard him correctly. But before she could say anything, Major Golubev tipped his hat and walked away from the school.

* * *

Oksana was sitting alone in the dark of her office, the sickly blue glow of the phone lighting her face. Her eyes were heavy with exhaustion.

All afternoon she had watched the video of enemy missiles hitting the Administration building in a neighbouring city. Over and over the footage flashed across her screen. Each time the missile hit with equal precision. Each time the terror seemed to only magnify.

Lying on her desk was the now-banned Homeland flag. Oksana had taken it down earlier and folded it neatly, hoping it wouldn't fall into the hands of Mikhailovich's goons if they ever came again. She picked up the yellow and blue flag; the soft silk gave her comfort.

Though she was alone in her office, she shared the same horror as everyone else watching the terror unfold in her country. All were sending the same messages of shock, anger and grief.

Oksana knew the building in the video intimately. It was a place she had travelled as a child and young adult. She could picture summers eating ice cream, looking up at the stunning clocktower while the adults talked politics and life. In her mind's eye, she could hear her mother chastising her as she leapt between cobblestones with Dmytro.

"If you touch a crack, you'll break your back!" she had cackled.

The video played again in her hand. And again. The endless loop showing what had happened only hours earlier in the exact same place Oksana had spent fooling around with her brother all those years ago.

There it was, like a movie. Like a video game. A large group of happy children and parents walking the streets, carrying bags of groceries, before they disappeared into a flash of light, smoke, rubble and twisted metal. Gone.

Though she wanted to cry, she couldn't. Not yet.

This is terrorism, Oksana thought to herself. What else was there to call such evil?

Oksana posted messages of protest across various platforms. It seemed pointless to her, but what else could she do but scream into the digital void with her fellow citizens?

Outside her office window, she watched the new telecommunications workers climb the signal tower. Sent from the East, Oksana had seen them working in other parts of the city too. Across the river, she could see the heavily armed soldiers standing atop the city dam. The roads to the entire industrial precinct, including her own offices, were now blocked with tanks and heavy equipment. *New management*, she thought bitterly.

Though it was early in the autumn season, a light snow began to fall. The white flakes gave the landscape an eerie, serene quality.

As she placed the flag neatly into her rucksack, Oksana looked at her phone. The signal was dead.

CHAPTER 4

The skies! *The skies are killing us! We are dying on the ground! You must close our skies!*

Will they close them? Surely, they can see.

Doors were knocked on. Houses searched. Interrogations.

First, looking for the sons. Sometimes, coming for the daughters. Horrors taken to shallow graves.

"We know he is here. We know he is a veteran. It will be easier for him to cooperate. Tell us where he is, old man. Tell us!"

A father's face is smashed with the butt of a machine rifle. A mother cries, shielding his body with her own. Begging for absolution. Begging to disappear.

All performed in the service of madness. A drunk Father acting in the name of the Mother. A history co-opted, perverted. *This is your liberty.*

The fighting had been furious. Bombardment brutalising the country. Tanks advancing mercilessly to the Capital. Two hundred miles. One hundred miles. Fifty miles. Ten miles.

Erasing a culture as they went. Total victory was imminent.

But wars are two-way affairs. Explosions can be returned. Sometimes with interest.

Heroes hiding in the shadows wait patiently. Waiting. Waiting. Then come the javelins of fire. Heroes hurling relentlessly. Once quiet suburban streets descend into a hellscape of chaos.

Retribution comes in hot. The earth shakes.

In their shelters they listen. They cling to loved ones. To animals. But the Heroes record the madness they see and feel, too. Peering through windows and around corners they bravely hold their phones to the world.

They do so not for history or posterity.

In green shirts, they present their recordings as calls to action. To position the enemy. To position the world.

Surely, they will see? And then they will come. They must come.

Morning breaks upon the dread. A visual accompaniment to the night's deadly symphony.

Underneath destroyed bridges they gather. The survivors. Shivering in the winter's chill. Hiding from the rain. And the skies. They are the lucky ones.

Who is left?

I haven't seen him in days.

I think she went West. I pray she went West.

He has joined the armies, gone East.

My god, the children. The children.

God, help us. Someone, help us.

An old woman is held in the arms of her husband. A former submarine sailor for the Empire, he summons ancient strength to carry her. The nights are no longer tenable for them.

Last night, the explosions were too close, he says. It is safer now to walk in the open, risking hellfire, than to remain without her refrigerated medicine. The old couple must head West for desperately needed cancer medicine. There is a good hospital, their son tells them. They must try. Such are the choices that madness brings.

The broken and lucky file onto the yellow buses.

As their bus pulls away from the curb, the old soldier looks back to survey all that has been shattered. But they are heading to safety. The others will follow too.

The skies open again. This will be the last ride today.

In the occupied areas, the interrogations continue. Home to broken home.

"Are you Fascists? Why are you protecting the Fascists? Tell us. Tell us."

In free cities the lines at stores return. Bigger lines. But now the people line up for guns. All day long the men and women queue patiently, waiting for the latest delivery before marching to a post. Shock is turning to defiance. And defiance turns into seething anger.

Let them come. We will kill them where they stand. We will send them home in boxes. They will not take our home. Let them come.

The stories wash from East to West. Not even death can conceal the truth. The graves talk. People know.

As the lines grow, so does their confidence.

Give us guns. Let us fight. We will show you who is a Fascist.

A world still watching, still talking, moved tentatively East.

What is possible? How can we stop the madness?

While their countries debate what can be done, the bravest come on their own, eager to help. Some had been warning of this for years. Now it has come to pass.

Two grizzled Western soldiers carrying high-level equipment climb aboard a train heading East. They are not the first. Or the last. There is no fortune to be had. But some things are worth dying for.

In the night, on the outskirts of the Capital, a young soldier of the Motherland can be heard phoning home. "But, Mamma, they do not welcome us like we were told," he says. "There are no flowers. Tell Papa they are killing us."

And in the morning, there stands the Capital.

Beneath wide open skies, the Capital is there.

Surely, they can see?

CHAPTER 5

The Union meeting had been running for several hours before Oleksandr Abramovich rose to speak.

The packed Union Hall room was hot with frustration. Everyone present was exhausted, Oleksandr included.

Though it had been less than two weeks since the invasion, the lack of sleep and mounting stress were taking a toll on the members. And then there were the hours. The work itself was intense at the best of times. It was high stakes, requiring equally high levels of technical precision. Only now, there was no relief at all.

Large parts of the workforce had left town at the outbreak of war, before the Invaders had arrived in the city. Anyone who could get West, did. The young men and women had gone East to fight, or melted into the nearby forests awaiting a moment where they could press their advantage.

This left the bare minimum of staff to run the operations of the nuclear plant and all its supporting infrastructure. That meant those remaining were, in effect, prisoners of war and servants of public safety in equal measure. One false move, one tired mistake would mean disaster.

As the Union leader, Oksana knew around-the-clock shifts with skeleton crews would be unacceptable in normal times. A strike with associated demands for pay rises and additional crews would be brewing, if not already underway. What's more, Oksana herself would be leading the charge or agitating for change.

However, any strike involving a nuclear facility would be carefully negotiated with the plant management, the Mayor, local regulators and the members themselves to ensure maximum safety of the facilities. Union members were tough, but they weren't reckless fools.

But for workers and their families, refusing to work now would be risking far more than food on the table. A failure in the plant would mean utter catastrophe. And those on the other side? Well, they had made it clear they were prepared to contemplate the unthinkable.

It was a diabolical situation. They were all trapped.

Chairing the meeting, Oksana had seen the warning signs before. The rows of seats were filled with an unhappy cohort of technicians, engineers, scientists, cleaners and operators. All were facing the large wooden lectern at the front of the Hall from which Oksana was directing proceedings.

According to Oksana's roll, there were 1,907 members in attendance. Though not every member was in attendance – a crew was still working the night shift – the number was down from a peak workforce figure of 4,150, well below the accepted safe operating threshold of 2,500.

A wooden gavel in her hand, Oksana surveyed the crowd. Downturned faces, furrowed brows, folded arms. *Hopefully not closed minds*, Oksana thought to herself.

And why *wouldn't* they be unhappy? Workers joined Unions for protection, improved conditions and safety at work. Through their memberships they rightly expected their collective strength to prevent what they were now experiencing. Now they were back where it all began for earlier generations: work to death, or be put to death. Life under the hammer – or the gun – was not the sort of thing to inspire hope or high performance at any time, let alone now.

Oksana looked at the words emblazoned on the wall at the back of the room in large, metal signage: *The Power of Unity*. Underneath was the mounted crest of the Industrial Workers' Union. The words had never been more true, nor felt more empty, than right now.

If nothing else, Oksana knew a meeting of this length made people hungry and grumpy. And hungry, grumpy people weren't much good for any sort of conversation. But going home and cooling off was not an option. No, twenty-three speakers and ninety-six minutes into the meeting, it would have to be debated. Right here and now. There was no escape.

Amidst the anger, a hopelessness hung in the air too.

In their hearts, everyone knew that no matter what was resolved by the rules of Union debate – no matter how many words expended, motions proposed, or votes taken – nothing would change. Motherfication of their city would continue. Family and friends would die. And the work would remain. It was the truth. And it was soul destroying.

Oksana felt for her brothers and sisters. Even though she was equally a prisoner, perhaps more so, she felt responsible for the situation. She knew genuine solutions were impossible, but as the Union Secretary, it was impossible not to feel the burden of leadership.

As Oleksandr rose to his full six feet, the plastic chair he'd been sitting on tipped over behind him, causing a hush to fall over the agitated and murmuring crowd. Oleksandr's hair, grey but impressively thick for a man in his early sixties, fell across his weathered and lined brow. He was dressed in the same blue overalls as his colleagues, with high-visibility reflective panels on his still-broad chest, back and shoulders. On his left arm, he bore the yellow sash that had become prominently displayed by locals around the city.

Small acts of defiance and civic pride were all they had for now. And they mattered. They certainly helped with local morale, but there was an added benefit. Like a pebble in the shoe, they slowly ate away at the enemy's resolve by letting them know they were surrounded by friendly enemies. Or at least, that was the theory.

Oleksandr was a long-time servant of the plant and the Union. Like many men his age, he had known no other job, town or life. His first job was helping to construct the plant with his father when it was commissioned decades ago, on the Empire's watch. Oleksandr had then studied at the local technical college to learn the processes and underpinning nuclear science before eventually obtaining a PhD in Physics. He took immense pride and satisfaction in his life's work. Most powerfully, Oleksandr been present the day of The Accident and helped rebuild the newer, modern facility they all worked in today.

Oksana knew Oleksandr's words carried weight with Union members. In many ways, he *was* the nuclear plant. His experience, history and reputation for honesty made him an almost fatherlike figure amongst the membership. A big strapping man, he did not speak without purpose.

And just like everyone else, Oksana had always looked up to Oleksandr. She'd spent summers playing with his daughters, Yulia and Vikka. As a long-time friend of her father, Timofei, Oleksandr had made sure Oksana was looked after when she started at the plant well after her father had passed. Though he never communicated it to her, Oksana knew the respect, perhaps reverence, Oleksandr had for Timofei.

Thanks to Oleksandr's hawkish oversight, there was none of the usual hazing or ritualised nonsense that would be expected of new recruits. Oleksandr made sure of it.

But this closeness had not prevented Oksana from challenging, and then defeating, Oleksandr for the role of Union Secretary at the previous year's Union elections.

When the long-term Union head, Zhenya Zukinov, had retired, most members assumed that Oleksandr would be his successor. He was the natural leader of the group and had the years of experience to seamlessly step into the role. In fact, such was his command of the Union members, he could have defeated Zhenya years earlier if the ambition struck him.

But Oksana was ambitious herself. Even as the elections approached, she didn't think the obvious natural order could be disrupted. Perhaps one day she could be leader of the Union, following in her father's famous footsteps, but not yet.

Surveying the room, Oksana thought back to that fateful day when Zhenya called her into his office.

Zhenya explained that, though most people considered Oleksandr his likely successor, he intended to nominate Oksana for the role. He knew this would come as a shock, but his mind was made up: she was the future. Should Oksana accept the nomination – which he insisted she must – Zhenya promised to pledge his support and considerable fundraising skills to her for the upcoming campaign.

"In many ways, my dear girl, this is a restoration of the

true order of things," Zhenya began. "Your father made this Union what it is. He made this city what it is. He gave his life to protect us during The Accident. And I – well, I would not have been in this role at all if Timofei was still with us . . ." he had said, trailing off.

Though she protested lightly, in truth it did not take much to persuade Oksana to agree to Zhenya's proposition. Somehow, it felt right to her.

The contest between Oksana and Oleksandr was close. But a combination of Zhenya's support and Oksana's own Union pedigree got her over the line. It was a famous victory.

To be the head of the Union at such a young age was an extraordinary achievement. But Zhenya had identified Oksana's prodigious talent from the beginning. And deep down so had Oleksandr. She was her father's daughter, after all.

Her ability to negotiate record pay rises with minimal stoppages had already set her well above her contemporaries. But the most impressive feat of all, thanks to her doctoral work, was the way Oksana could identify major process innovations at the plant that dramatically lifted energy productivity, reduced costs and boosted profits.

Things like this made the members, even the sceptical ones, admire Oksana. When things got tough, they looked to her, which was why Zhenya had wanted to elevate Oksana in the first place.

Without Zhenya none of this would have been possible,

Oksana thought as she looked around the Union Hall. And now he was gone. Though he'd hidden it at the time, Zhenya was dying from the town's curse. Like so many before him, the disease would eat him from the inside within the year. Taken before his time, the election of Oksana into the Secretary's position would be Zhenya's final act of solidarity.

While the Union ballot was conducted as amicably as possible, things were never quite the same between Oksana and Oleksandr. As sometimes happens, a frost grew between the victor and the vanquished. It was sad. But this too was the natural order of things.

The booming voice of Oleksandr drew Oksana back into the present.

The large man was rising to respond to an earlier address from Nikita, another of the plant's senior workplace leaders. Nikita had proposed a general strike and a refusal to work until certain demands were met. Invoking the history of The Accident, the man reminded those in attendance that work could not possibly continue as it was without a major safety incident of some kind. The exhaustion everyone was experiencing would inevitability lead to mistakes with potentially dire consequences. In fact, it was a miracle something hadn't happened already, he said.

"And without us, let us not forget, they die too! These bastards, they will be forced to negotiate once they understand the stakes! It is the only thing that makes sense," Nikita concluded.

His comments had received a strong round of applause

from the assembled members. Impassioned and logical, Nikita's words had captured the mood of the assembled membership.

Oleksandr began his right of reply. "The words of Brother Nikita are compelling. They are courageous. They are just. But, my brothers and sisters, they are wrong. And, what's more, you all know them to be wrong."

The crowd began to murmur amongst themselves. This wasn't what they were expecting from their almost-leader.

"To negotiate successfully," Oleksandr continued, "one must have leverage. Perhaps we have some leverage over our oppressors, as Brother Nikita has suggested. Perhaps, Madam Secretary Shevchenko could put forward your valid concerns with sufficient confidence that our unity and strength could persuade those opposite to agree to our demands. But to negotiate, one must also have honesty and goodwill on both sides.

"What could possibly give Brother Nikita confidence," he began to ask the crowd, "what could give *any* of us confidence that these proposed negotiations, being so resolutely debated in this hallowed Hall, would even be contemplated by the Invaders? You have seen their brutality. I can only presume Brother Nikita was asleep when the Invaders fired upon the facility as they arrived. Those of you who have seen what can happen when things go awry, who were alive during The Accident, tell me: did your blood not run cold? Did you not fear the worst as flames appeared next to the cooling towers? Did you not think of your loved ones?

"Comrades, these people are not for turning or accommodating, and so it is we who must turn. You have all seen the indifference to life on both sides. No, it was so-called negotiations and meaningless words from politicians that drew us into this pointless and horrific endeavour. And now what do we have? Sisters killing brothers. Brothers killing sisters. A family at war."

The crowd murmured. Oleksandr continued on.

"Those of us in this room have a most sacred task ahead of us. We have a duty to protect our city and to protect those who live here, just as we always have. None of us asked for this new burden, it is true. But it is incumbent upon us all to do what we must to save the lives of those we can."

"And so, you would have us surrender to this butchery and treachery?" a younger man yelled from the back of the room.

Oksana raised her hand to restore order to debate. But before she could use her gavel, Oleksandr turned to address the man.

"Surrender? Tell me, Brother, to what are we surrendering, and to whom? Will ending the conflict change who lives here? Will it change our history? No, of course not. Instead, we die in service of the vanity of others. Those who attack us and those who ask us to fight in service of their own ambitions, they have no place here."

"So you *do* wish to surrender!" the young man yelled.

"Tell me – those who fight and die, are they seeing their bravery honoured with negotiations?" Oleksandr asked. "No, the destruction continues. Why would these discussions be any different? How would this attempt at negotiation via industrial muscle help us avoid more death and, perhaps, our final destruction? Can you give such an assurance to those who would be caught in the ashes?"

Oksana could feel the tension rising in the room. Union members, usually adept at decorum and respecting the rights of the speaker, began to look at one another, somewhat shocked at what they were hearing. Others began to interject.

"We did not ask for this War or this Invasion!" a middle-aged woman yelled. "We did not ask to be held as prisoners here! How else can we resist this madness?"

"And, Sister, who is it we die for? Who is it we are asked to kill? Tell me, who?" Oleksandr retorted. "And what of us who just want peace? What of us who have friends and family in the Motherland? What of relationships that go back into blood and soil and a history not written in any books? What of this shared past that does not respect lines on a map?"

"We all want peace, you fool!" a man yelled.

"Let him speak! He speaks sense!" yelled another.

"Order!" screamed Oksana as she hammered her gavel repeatedly.

Oleksandr knew the room was shifting against him, but he persevered. With the stakes as high as they were, he would not leave this world wondering if he could have stopped it all, even if it meant losing friends along the way.

"I assure you, my dear Brothers and Sisters, I feel your pain. I feel the death of those who have fallen acutely. Please do not take my words as those of a defeatist, but of a realist. Hear my words as the triumph of experience over hope."

The crowd, unruly only a few seconds before, grew still as they listened.

"How many new starts have we seen?" Oleksandr said. "I was there when the Empire's Wall fell. I was there during the March of Colours. I filled the square during the Revolution of Respect. I stood shoulder to shoulder with some of you in this very room and resisted the pummelling from the corrupted guards of our corrupted former president. I too hoped for a new future. But this promised future has not come. And those of you who still wait, I ask you, what respect have they for you? They take you for fools and play a game that is rigged for themselves."

He glanced intently into the eyes of his fellow Union members across the Hall. "No, we must look after one another here. It is all that matters. Here we have control. Here we can live in peace."

Oleksandr paused, taking a second to gather his thoughts before raising his voice to match the moment.

"And to those of you who talk of fighting and resisting – tell me, how many of you have seen combat? How many of you have seen death? I have seen it. I have seen its fury. I have seen its cutting indifference. I was there when the Empire was defeated on the battlefield many decades ago, before the Wall fell. I know the pain of foolish endeavour and military overreach – and I also know the folly of death in pursuit of a frivolous and rose-coloured resistance."

"But they seek to erase us!" yelled a young man, this time closer to Oleksandr. "These murderers come not just for our heads. They come for our history. How many more years must we suffer these indignities? Have you forgotten the Great Famine of last century?"

The old man sensed the danger. The room was closing in. The air was going out.

"Brother Oleksandr, your time is at an end. Please conclude," Oksana said, dropping her gavel to the lectern with authority.

Turning to the Chair, Oleksandr nodded dutifully. "I will conclude, Madam Secretary." He looked again at the crowd. "My Brothers and Sisters, like all of you, I have spoken the Mother tongue for my whole life. I also honour our Native tongue and our Native history here in the Homeland. But lines on a map are meaningless. This is how it has always been here. And this is how it will remain. Families and cultures living as they must, side by side. A complex history that only those on the ground can truly understand. But know this, my friends. Regardless of their stripe, or their method, or ideology, all governments and all who aspire to the vanity of leadership are the same."

Oleksandr removed his yellow sash and held it aloft to the crowd. "The colours may change. But nothing changes. Nothing! And you are fools to believe otherwise."

More interjectors began to yell. Oksana stood to her feet and called for order. Now, she knew, was the time to end the meeting. "Brother Oleksandr will resume his seat. His time has expired," she said.

Amidst the murmuring, and before Oksana could officially close the meeting, she saw a young, thin man named Viktor toward the back of the room stand to his feet and begin to speak.

"Brother Olek is right! Don't you see, you fools? This madwoman is taking us to our deaths like that incompetent father of hers. Only this time, she plans to finish the job!" screamed Viktor while pointing towards Oksana, seated at the front of the room.

Immediately, the entire room snapped its attention to look at Viktor, whose neck was pulsing with anger and fear. Oksana sat in her seat, frozen in shocked silence.

But Viktor wasn't done. "We all know what happened all those years ago. We have read the reports. This town was nearly wiped from the map because of Timofei Shevchenko. And now you ask us all to follow this utter lightweight to our certain doom? Well, I will have no part of it. None."

"Shut up, you moron! Timofei Shevchenko is a hero!" an older man shouted from nearby.

"Hero?" Viktor scoffed. "Please. He is an international embarrassment. One of the only engineers to ever preside over a partial nuclear meltdown anywhere in the world. And it happened, right here. Because of his mistakes, people died and continue to die. And this ineptitude, like the poison he unleashed? Well, it is in the bloodstream. To live under her heel, my Brothers and Sisters, would be a mistake."

Suddenly, the young man was brought to the ground with a crashing *thud* that knocked over numerous chairs and sent nearby Union members scattering.

"I was there! *I was there*!" screamed Oleksandr as he pinned Viktor to the ground by the throat, his right arm clenched high above, ready to sink into the man's skull.

Before any genuine violence could occur, Union members rushed to the scene in a scrum of humanity. Most of their attention was on subduing Oleksandr, who was an ogre of rage.

"Get off me, you old thug! Have you lost your mind?" yelled Viktor as he clambered to his feet and away from the clutches of Oleksandr, who was still struggling to shake free from the several men holding his arms and shoulders.

"Let me go!" screamed Oleksandr.

Having regained his feet, Viktor quickly made his way through the gawking onlookers to the exit at the back of the room.

"Go on. Run, you coward! Run! You forget I know where you work for a living!" Oleksandr called after him.

With Viktor out of sight, Oleksandr instantly began to calm down. With the hulking man no longer thrashing, the men deemed it safe to let Oleksandr go.

"*Have* you lost your mind?" asked Nikita.

Oleksandr was a little sheepish, as he saw Nikita had been one of the men holding him during his minute of madness.

"No more than usual, Brother Nikita. No more than usual," said Oleksandr, straightening his clothes.

"Are you alright, Olek?" Nikita asked.

"I am, I am. It's this new generation. They talk of what they do not know."

"It was ever thus."

"Perhaps, perhaps . . ." Oleksandr trailed off, lost in his thoughts.

Rattled by what had just happened, Oksana noted the time and was thankful she could justifiably conclude the proceedings. With no further debate to be allowed, a motion for future deliberations was hastily moved and passed, alongside Oksana's promise to raise the overall concerns of the workforce with the new "management". With the short smack of her gavel, the meeting was concluded.

As the grumbling and now quite shocked crowd of Union members filed out of the room, Oksana stared at Oleksandr, who was quietly speaking with some concerned friends and supporters.

Unity had been maintained. But only just. And perhaps for not much longer.

* * *

Outside the Union Hall, it was dark. A light snow was falling across the city.

Oleksandr was smoking alone when Oksana finally emerged from the building, turning to lock the doors behind her.

"I am sorry, Madam Secretary," Oleksandr said.

Still on edge, Oksana spun quickly on her heels to face the voice coming from the dark.

"Relax, Oksana, relax. It's Olek," he said with a soothing voice, stepping into the weak light of the nearby lamppost.

Oksana breathed a sigh of relief. Her long, hot exhale into the frigid air caused a pocket of a steam to flow from her face.

"That was quite a meeting, huh?" Oleksandr said with an exhale of his cigarette.

"That's one way of putting it."

"I'm . . . I'm sorry for losing my cool in there. I was—"

"Unprofessional? Nuts? A total *baniak*?" Oksana interjected.

"Out of line," Oleksandr said with a grin.

"It's okay. You were just saying what I was thinking. I'm just upset you didn't clobber that rat," Oksana chuckled.

"The younger me would have!" Oleksandr declared with a half-hearted effort at shadow boxing.

Oksana laughed again.

The crinkled mirth left the old man's eyes as his face grew smooth and serious. "I know you did not want me to speak, but I felt I had to. I hope you understand."

She stood silent for a moment, contemplating her next words. She took a half step towards Oleksandr. "It is nothing. You had to say your piece, I understand. But you must understand that none of us want this. Even those who want to fight don't wish for death. We want to wish this all away as much as you do. But wishing it away doesn't make it any less true. Nobody wants this, Olek. Nobody wants to see people die."

"Nobody ever does. And yet it always comes. That's the grim certainty of the matter. I can't help but look at you, and even my dearest granddaughter – I want none of this for you. None of it. You all have so much life left. And you don't know how bad it can get."

"We know. Truly, we do. And how is little Katya?"

"Not so little anymore. She's almost my height! And quite the athlete. The old Empire would have made a champion of her!" Oleksnadr laughed.

"There's still time," Oksana said, gently smiling. "We are glad to have you."

Oleksandr drew deeply on his cigarette, deep in thought.

"As for that idiot Viktor . . . well, I just couldn't have him spreading lies . . ."

An awkward pause filled the space between them.

"Your father . . ."

"It's okay, Olek, truly." She reached to touch Oleksandr's arm. "It's late. We best beat curfew."

"You go ahead, I need to clear my head a little," the old man said as he leaned against the lamppost and lit a fresh cigarette.

She paused for a moment before she turned to leave. "Good night, Olek."

"Madam Secretary!" Oleksandr called after Oksana, who stopped to look over her shoulder. "You know, you are just like him."

Oksana smiled and nodded thankfully before continuing on into the night.

Alone, Oleksandr looked up at the bright night sky.

"You are just like him . . ." he said to himself.

* * *

Mikhailovich was sitting at what was now *his* large wooden desk in the Administration building when Oksana entered the room. The desk was meticulously appointed, with papers neatly stacked in trays. A single heavy fountain pen rested to Mikhailovich's left, while a glass of ice water sat on a wooden coaster to his right.

He had been waiting for her. Meetings between the two had been scheduled every day since the Occupation began.

"Miss Shevchenko, take a seat."

"I'm sorry to be late, but . . ." Oksana started.

"You had a Union meeting, yes?" Mikhailovich said calmly.

"Yes."

"We will get to the outcomes of that meeting shortly, but there is another matter that we must discuss." Mikhailovich opened the folder prepared in front of him. "These plant worker absentee numbers are unacceptable. Based on a rolling monthly average, recorded absentee hours are up – "

"Twenty-six point six per cent," Oksana interjected.

Still looking at the data in front of him, Mikhailovich raised his eyebrows before closing the folder and looking up at Oksana. "These are large numbers, no?"

"Perhaps."

"And what, then, is the meaning of them?"

"People are sick," Oksana said with a shrug.

"People are sick," Mikhailovich said before closing his eyes and inhaling deeply. "Miss Shevchenko, I have a job to do. I wish to do it and leave. You of all people can understand this, surely?" He opened his eyes again. "You would agree that our relations have been courteous and professional, yes?"

Oksana nodded. "I would grant you that, yes."

"Then please do not take me for a fool."

"I take you to be the man who dangerously and recklessly shelled a nuclear power facility – one of the largest of its kind in the world – before asking for its surrender," Oksana replied. "You may use whatever term you wish to describe that behaviour."

"And if I had wanted to destroy it, it would have happened, I assure you."

Oksana stared past Mikhailovich without response.

"Know this, Miss Shevchenko. Any failure to securely maintain this facility will end not in my professional embarrassment, but in the death of everyone and everything you hold near," he continued, his eyes narrowing. "And then I, having no further thought or regard for that eventuality, will return home to a hero's welcome."

"Yes. Yes, I know you will," Oksana said, her jaw stiffening.

Having felt his point was made, Mikhailovich's calm exterior returned. "Now, we are two professionals. Tell me how we reduce these numbers."

"Workers won't work without payment. Or fairness. And there are limits to how far humans can be pushed through fear or threat. Even the founders of the Old Empire worked that one out eventually."

Mikhailovich snorted. "Yes, perhaps that is true. While the Empire was of sound ambitions, its ideas and practices were dated and sadly defeated," he said, picking up the pen from the desk.

"Its ambitions?"

"But not this time," he continued, absently spinning the pen in his fingers. "We have learned from our errors. There are now capable men with a focus on proper execution." The words hung in the air before the officer slammed a hand to the table. "Now then, how are we to solve these issues between us?"

"Our members need an agreed day off every week, bonus payments in your currency and at least one non-local relief crew sourced from the East. These people need a rest," she replied.

He nodded slowly. "Very well, I will see that it is done."

Their business concluded, Mikhailovich opened another folder on his desk and began to study its content. "You may see yourself out."

Oksana stood and began to walk to the door.

"Oh, and Miss Shevchenko, please remember the uniforms are not to be supplemented with additional dressage," he said without looking up.

Oksana stopped and spun around.

"I trust you understand the concern," he began. "Should we have visitations, it would appear most improper. As you would know, these additions – while ever so clever – are breaches of the new flag Ordinances."

"Breaches how?" Oksana asked.

Mikhailovich paused in his work and looked up. "It would be wise, for all our sakes, not to test my patience, Miss Shevchenko."

Oksana nodded slowly. "And that is all?"

"That is all."

* * *

The next day at the plant, workers on the morning shift attended without the standard yellow sash.

In its place, each Union member was carrying a freshly painted golden lunchbox. Even a glum Oleksandr.

CHAPTER 6

A FORTY-MILE COLUMN of death snakes along the arteries of the Homeland. Heading for the heart, it carries its awful objective.

But cargo from the West has come. Finally. Slowly. Obstinately. But it is here. Precious weaponry. Not enough to turn the tide, but perhaps enough to stop it from drowning the innocent. Drones for the sky. Guns and shells for the ground. Sandbags added to the bravery of heroes. Guns for their glory. A fighting chance.

Against all odds, somehow, incredibly, the heart is protected. The snake is stopped in its tracks. Its head cut from its body, writhing, directionless. Those hungry to inflict revenge can sense their moment. And they do not miss. War's bitter victory is tasted.

But for every fleeting moment of success, the horrors are endless.

In the far limbs of the Homeland, the people are suffering unspeakably. The extermination continues.

Bombardment. Siege. Murder. Terror. Promised green corridors for humanitarian evacuations fail to materialise. Hours without warmth, food, water, medicine turn to days. And then to weeks.

A little boy dies of dehydration. *How can this happen today?*

None are spared. Entire cities killed. And all who remain are choking in the destruction.

And the theatre.

Did you see the theatre? How many were there when the bombs hit? Children butchered. Futures stolen. It is unthinkable, but it cannot be unseen. It happened. Today.

Eastern crematoriums on wheels can be seen from satellites. They insidiously trail behind the destruction being sown. They have been sent to hide their own dead. And to cover tracks.

In the West of the Homeland, the Invaders waver. Boys are no longer suffering delusions of grandeur.

Stranded without food, without munitions, without water, they pray for their own liberation. Divisions that exist only on paper are allocated equipment never purchased. Young men labour under a madman's certainty. Meanwhile, the thieves float on yachts.

Fight. Die. The Motherland needs you.

Pawns pressed forward from the East are driven back from the West. The fighting is intense. Souls are liberated from their bodies. Those left standing run.

The retreating soldiers carry a truth with them that must be destroyed.

"We have been lied to, Comrades."

"These orders make no sense, Mamma."

"We must have more cover, Captain."

"We do not have the equipment we need, General."

"All is progressing as planned, My Commander."

"The Fascists are losing, my fellow Comrades."

But the truth, it cannot be killed.

The Capital is still standing. The stubborn, simple truth of this is undeniable.

Incontrovertible, this truth will not be surrendered.

Her determination to persist can be seen by the entire world.

And like the heroes defending her, she is glorious.

CHAPTER 7

"AND HOW ARE the preparations for our Patriots' Day celebrations coming?" Mikhailovich asked.

He sat with Sokolov and Golubev in his office drinking whisky, the stars beginning to peek out behind the dark night sky. Mikhailovich was rocked back in his leather seat, a boot resting on the wooden surface of his desk. The heavy, crystal whisky glass was perched on his knee. He held it up and twisted it slowly with his fingers. Sokolov picked as his nails, as he typically did when he was disinterested.

"All proceeding as normal," said Sokolov, drawing back on his cigarette.

Golubev nodded his agreement while stirring his whisky and looking into the reflection of the dense crystal. He took a sip from the glass, oblivious to his superior's stare.

"'Normal' . . ." Mikhailovich said, looking at the two men. "And you are sure?"

Sokolov paused. "Yes, sir," he replied, blowing the smoke from his mouth a little more hastily.

"And what gives you such confidence?"

"Is there something I should know, Comrade Lieutenant General?" Sokolov said, drawing back on the last of his smoke. He squashed the butt in a nearby ashtray.

"I trust you are following the news?"

"I read the reports provided." Sokolov hit his chest pocket in search of his cigarette packet before realising it was in his right jacket pocket. He fished out the box, took out a cigarette and placed it in his mouth.

"And the news?" the Lieutenant General pressed.

Sokolov paused to light the cigarette. "I don't have time for such trivialities."

Golubev smirked before taking a sip of his whisky. "Trivialities?" he asked, turning to Sokolov.

"Then perhaps you are the man of letters at this table, Comrade Major Golubev?" said Mikhailovich, suddenly entertained.

Sensing danger in his tone, Golubev did not offer a response.

"Come now, are you both telling me you haven't heard the reports relating to the untimely death of General Hlinofsky?" Mikhailovich said, rocking forward suddenly in his seat and dropping his boots to the ground with a thud. "It is of course terribly sad news to lose a leader of General Hlinosky's capabilities," he continued, catching himself slightly. Even still, he could barely contain his enthusiasm regarding the death of a superior officer.

Sokolov nodded, suddenly understanding the probing of Mikhailovich and the direction he wished to take the conversation. Golubev took a sip from his whisky, watching both men.

Sokolov drew deeply on his cigarette before speaking. "You see, Comrade Lieutenant General, trivialities," he said with a long exhale.

Mikhailovich laughed heartily. "But with intrigue, Comrade Colonel!" he added, his finger pointed in the air.

"Naturally, this presents a major gap in our senior military command structure," said Sokolov. "One that will require some filling, I assume."

"Indeed, Colonel," Mikhailovich agreed. "Tell me, do either of you know what happened to our dear Comrade General?"

"I understand there was an ambush, sir," Sokolov replied, shrugging slightly.

"Well, those are the reports. But the truth is a little, shall we say, different," said Mikhailovich.

Sokolov frowned. "Different?"

"Well, an ambush suggests good planning on the part of the enemy. A well-executed ambush could, in most instances, not have been prevented."

Sokolov nodded his agreement. This was self-evidently true.

"No, it is my understanding that the General made a most foolish error," Mikhailovich continued. "One that cost the lives of him and his men."

"An error?" asked Sokolov.

"It seems the General failed to coordinate his air, sea and land forces for an integrated attack on the enemy. On the ground, he pressed too close behind the front lines with his own embedded command unit. And, most critically, he pushed his forces into an effective cul-de-sac – one located in a major urban area, with multiple high points of defence for the enemy. All of this was done, most incredibly, without the standard preceding artillery bombardment."

Mikhailovich paused. He looked at both men with the eagerness of a schoolboy. "It was a turkey shoot!" he continued, setting his glass down almost gleefully before either man could respond.

"That's a lot of Christmas dinners," said Sokolov, blowing smoke in the air.

Mikhailovich laughed loudly, slapping his thigh with good humour.

"He was a man I served with," said Golubev without looking up from his glass.

Both Mikhailovich and Sokolov turned to look at Golubev. It was almost like both men had forgotten he was there.

"We were in the academy together. He fought with distinction for the Empire. A fine soldier," Golubev said quietly before turning to Mikhailovich and raising his glass.

Mikhailovich's face reddened slightly.

"We *all* served with him, Comrade Major," said Sokolov, having noticed the Lieutenant General's embarrassment.

"They did too, those poor bastards who died today. They were the last . . ." Golubev trailed off, filling his glass with more whisky from the bottle sitting on the edge of the desk.

Sokolov shot his eyes at Golubev, chastising him silently for his impertinence. Golubev knew full well what sort of temper Mikhailovich had, Sokolov thought to himself.

Despite the attention, Golubev did not dare look up from his task. He knew Sokolov was staring at him. But at this point, he didn't care. He had said what he said. And he meant it. Having poured the glass perfectly, he sat back in his chair without looking in the direction of either Sokolov or Mikhailovich.

In any event, Sokolov decided to come to his old friend's aid by trying to defuse the highly uncomfortable and potentially explosive situation. "Yes, Major, but of course, as you would know, Comrade Lieutenant General is correct in his assessment. The events described are not correct battlefield procedure or modern warfare planning. Even a *Major* would know how to avoid a trap like this, wouldn't you agree?"

Golubev, returning to his whisky, nodded in slow

agreement. Though he was sickened by Sokolov's indulging of Mikhailovich, he knew better than to push his luck any further.

"I have to say, gentlemen, it is a curious thing – how a senior man of General Hlinofsky's status came to be so close to the frontlines is odd, to say the least. It appears wasteful," said Mikhailovich, almost rhetorically.

"Well, one man's waste is another's treasure, Lieutenant General," said Sokolov, raising his glass ever so slightly.

"I thought those orders and plans came directly from The Commander," said Golubev.

This comment cut the conversation dead for a long beat. Even Mikhailovich looked uncomfortable at the raw truth of it.

The Lieutenant General broke the silence. "Yes, perhaps that is so. But as we know, even with a perfect plan, the execution is always the key. But in this instance it wasn't the procedure that was the problem, gentlemen. No, it was the will to win. The will to do whatever it takes. Regrettably, our dearly departed Comrade General was too kind to the Fascists, and they took advantage of this weakness, of his humanity in old age. History proves that brutality of the kind we are facing today can only be defeated with an even greater and more relentless brutality." As he finished, he thumped the table slightly with his knuckles for effect.

"Yes, but experience also shows that war is never fought on paper," said Golubev before adding, "Sir," just in time to evade Sokolov's narrowing eyes.

"Quite. Which brings me back to the subject of Patriots' Day," Mikhailovich said, switching gears. He rocked back in his chair, resuming his leisurely position from earlier. His boots landed closely to where Golubev had been resting his glass. "For obvious reasons, you can understand my interest in avoiding ambush or embarrassment on this most holy of days for the Motherland. This is, after all, a celebration of our finest victory over the Nazis during the Great Patriotic War."

"Of course, sir," said Sokolov before shooting Golubev a warning from the sides of his eyes.

Golubev took the hint. "Naturally," he agreed.

"So, tell me then, how are you planning to avoid any such issues?" asked Mikhailovich.

"Everything is planned," Sokolov assured him. "We will have the manpower we need. There will be crowd control. We are monitoring communication channels, and there have been no signs of local resistance."

"No signs?" said Mikhailovich, raising his eyebrows.

"No signs of *violent* resistance," Sokolov corrected himself.

"My sources, they tell me that there may be trouble afoot," said Mikhailovich.

"Sources?" said Golubev with slight surprise before he could stop himself. It was highly improper to question a commanding officer about his intelligence sources.

"An expression, Golubev. In plain terms, I understand

there is a resistance movement in this town. We have all seen it with our very eyes, yes? Beyond that, not all briefings are declassified to your level, Comrade Major."

"Yes, sir, that is well understood," said Sokolov. "But the Major and I cannot help if you do not trust us with this information." He was annoyed at Golubev, but the old intelligence man in him was desperate to know more.

Mikhailovich conceded. "Very well, it is of no great importance. Intelligence reports indicate that there has been heightened resistance activity in the city. It would appear the Fascists are still actively operating inside the city limits. They are coordinating with Fascist armies and Fascist government officials.

"I am reliably informed that there is a sophisticated Fascist cell operating locally, detailing our activities here back to their superiors," he continued. "This is of course unacceptable to the Motherland. Most of all, it is unacceptable to me. Our orders – *your* orders – are to find this cell and destroy it. With the death of General Hlinofsky, you both no doubt understand why I – we – simply must succeed in our mission. Failure is not an option"

Sokolov nodded. "We can do that. It is a simple matter of hunting to kill. If you can share the intelligence reports, I am confident we can draw this Fascist infestation out and eradicate it like the pestilence it is."

Drinking from his glass, Mikhailovich did not

acknowledge Sokolov's request. He appeared to be contemplating something else. He paused before answering his comrade. "Then there are the ongoing issues relating to displays of Nativist colours and breaches of the identification Ordinances," he said, his eyes narrowing slightly.

"Yes, yes, I have seen this, of course," said Sokolov. "And then there is the matter of Nativist language, and the persistent use of Nativist phrases of solidarity." He hoped to get ahead of Mikhailovich's thoughts. He was smoking a little more energetically.

"But how are we to ban colours and words?" asked Golubev, injecting himself into the conversation. "Surely this is setting ourselves up to fail. For every one you destroy, three will spring up in its place." Golubev's long history in dealing with counter-insurgencies and military intelligence in the Old Empire had taught him that repressing such movements only gave them more legitimacy.

Sokolov paused slightly, letting out a slow exhale. "Perhaps we cannot ban them in their entirety. But we can, shall we say, strongly discourage the practice."

"Are we not already doing so?" Golubev retorted. "I fail to see what more can be done. The appropriate bans already exist. There are no Nativist flags flying. The Motherland's flag, The Commander's image, our currency, our language – it is all in place. We are ubiquitous."

Mikhailovich smiled. "I've told you, Comrade Major, we

are yet to institute the necessary levels of brutality to generate compliance."

"And what then is necessary, Comrade Lieutenant General?" asked Golubev, even though he already understood the meaning of such a phrase.

"Let your vast experience be your guide, Comrade Major," said Mikhailovich with a sneer.

Sensing Mikhailovich's growing impatience, Sokolov sought to end the conversation. "We will create the framework to drive compliance in the community. And it *will* be enforced."

"With necessary brutality," Mikhailovich added.

"Naturally," Sokolov agreed.

"Flies and honey . . ." muttered Golubev under his breath.

Mikhailovich's head snapped to attention. Sokolov rolled his eyes in exasperation at his friend, who seemingly had a professional death wish. Or worse.

"Come now, Major," barked Mikhailovich. "Do not deprive us of your stellar insights. Speak up. You are among friends, are you not?" He swept his hands across the room for theatrical effect.

Golubev sipped from his glass and paused for a moment. He looked at Mikhailovich squarely. "I *said*, flies are attracted to honey. Fear will only take us so far in the end. If we are to rule the people here, or at least create compliance, they will demand natural justice. We must be careful not to overreach.

History tells us a people will resist things that are, or appear to be, unjust."

Mikhailovich snorted. "What is natural and what is just are not the same, Major. Consider that it is natural for your fly to be attracted to horse shit. And then, equally, it is natural for this same fly to be eaten by a frog. And if that frog hopped away rather satisfied, only to be squashed on the road by my passing truck, why, that is a most natural act too." He leaned across the table. "And do you know what the filthy horse shit, the pesky fly, the temporarily satisfied frog and the conquering truck all have in common?"

"No, sir, I do not."

"None of them have a say in what is just. And all of them answer to me."

Mikhailovich paused to make certain his message had been received before continuing. Golubev did not dare speak.

"In the end, there are only two things that matter," said Mikhailovich, looking directly at Golubev. "Our objectives and our determination. I assure you, I will achieve our objectives and my assignment, come what may. My determination in these matters should not be doubted, not for a single second. I will be as kind, or as brutal, to these people as required. You needn't fear that, my dear Major."

An awkward silence filled the room.

"But," Mikhailovich continued, "I defer to your experience in these matters and trust you both to deal with these trifling problems with the appropriate method."

"It will be done," Sokolov affirmed, looking at Golubev sternly.

"Good," Mikhailovich said, his eyes flashing at the door. "Good night, gentlemen."

Golubev understood the conversation, such as it was, was over.

The meeting adjourned.

* * *

Walking from the room, Golubev silently kicked himself for having spoken so freely. *A little too much whisky*, he thought.

War always made him drink more. Wars like this, *much* more. Golubev thought of his wife back home. Valentyna would not approve of the drinking, that was for sure.

Even the idea of bickering with his wife made Golubev miss home and all its creature comforts. The smell of coffee in the morning. A walk to the park. A movie on the weekend. Suddenly, these all seemed lavish and unattainable.

Golubev was not someone who enjoyed the road, or even battle. Finding them distasteful, Golubev was never one for confirmed kill counts or other measures of military vanity. Killing was part of the job, certainly, but not to be admired.

For Golubev's entire career, his colleagues had identified this failure to truly love the army as the reason he was prevented from advancing as fast as his contemporaries. Men like Sokolov or Hlinovsky – or the scores of others he'd beaten as the top graduate at the Officer's Academy eons ago – they all outranked him. Even the kids he had mentored had to be saluted these days.

From time to time this rankled Golubev, but what was there to love about the army? Discipline was certainly admirable. The ability to carve out a good life, that was not to be taken for granted.

But surely an army was a necessary evil. Wouldn't it be better if the army was never needed at all?

These wistful, drunken thoughts preoccupied Golubev as he walked onto the quiet city street outside the military headquarters. Though curfew had not taken effect, most people had already gone indoors as whatever passed for nightlife was long gone. The need to protect from Homeland bombing raids meant the city's lights were off. Though, in the era of laser-guided missiles, this tactical measure seemed a little dated in Golubev's eyes.

Without the usual sirens and scramble of overhead activity, it was almost possible for Golubev to imagine the War wasn't happening. Standing in the darkness, he felt alone and at peace.

Despite the late autumn season, it was mild enough for Golubev to walk back to the barracks. The snow had been threatening but had not meaningfully fallen yet.

Looking up to the sky as he walked, he realised he

hadn't seen the stars shimmer like this since he was a small boy growing up in the Central West of the Old Empire. His father, an intelligence officer, had moved around with deployments as required, taking Golubev, his mother and three brothers along. Golubev's childhood memories made cities like Heryvin almost seem more like home than where he lived now.

Golubev was still looking in the sky when he bumped into a man who had been standing against a lamppost.

"Careful, you idiot," came a gruff voice.

Startled, Golubev pulled the flashlight from his belt, but not his gun. He placed the bright, circular light on the face of a burly older man dressed in blue overalls.

Oleksandr, a cigarette dangling from his mouth, placed his hands in the air to indicate he was not a threat.

"Calm down, Sasha. You'll kill someone with that thing. Or catch some fireflies," said Oleksandr, squinting into the bright light beam shooting into his face.

"What did you say?" said Golubev.

"I said you'd catch some fireflies," said Oleksandr.

"What do you mean by that?" said Golubev, walking forward slightly.

"Jesus, I meant the fireflies will come to your flashlight. When did you get so on edge?" said Oleksandr, attempting to lighten the mood.

"Oh, I don't know, Olek, maybe you've noticed the War?" said Golubev, turning the light down to the ground.

"Oh. Right. The War." He paused, as though in deep thought. "But, Sasha, how else would I have seen you after all these years?" he said with a smile.

Golubev laughed at the absurdity from his old friend.

"I mean, you never call, you never write . . ." said Oleksandr, warming into the theme of his joke.

"Okay, okay! Listen, I am already married. The job of putting me into an early grave is taken, so you'll need to find something else to occupy yourself with, you old Cossack fool."

"I think the queue is growing on that one by the day. For both of us!"

Both men started laughing. It relieved whatever lingering tension remained in the air.

Oleksandr offered a cigarette, which Golubev accepted.

"It has been a long time, Olek," Golubev said as Oleksandr reached out with a lighter.

Oleksander sparked his friend's cigarette to life. Even with the torch beam shining, the bright flash of the flint and flame lit up the darkness of the night sky. "It has. How many years?"

"At the last reunion. What was that, ten years ago now?" said Golubev. He put the cigarette to his lips and took a long drag.

"Yes, the last one. You're right. Maybe eleven," Oleksandr agreed. "You were so drunk! You forgot how to get yourself home," he continued, laughing at Golubev.

"I told you – I'm married. It can be pleasant to forget occasionally!"

Both men laughed again, like only old friends can.

The laughter eased into a comfortable silence. "Those of us who served in the Empire's godforsaken war in Afghanistan all those years ago, we need to stick together. Even when people try and pull us apart."

"Even then," said Golubev.

Oleksandr drew back heavily on his cigarette before blowing smoke into the air. Looking at the moon, he contemplated the situation. Never in his wildest imagination had he thought he would cross paths with his old friend under such trying circumstances. "Do you remember signing up together when they came to town? What did they say? 'Fortune and glory'? For the Empire? What nonsense did they sell us on?"

"The same things they're saying today, I should think," Golubev replied.

"You would know. Aren't you drafting the recruitment posters now?" Oleksandr laughed.

Golubev smiled weakly. Oleksandr realised he had pushed a raw nerve by accident.

"And how is that sneaky bastard, Sokolov?" the Union man asked. "He's barely looked me in the eye since he arrived."

"Don't worry, he's watching you. I think he's actually inside that lamppost."

Both men laughed heartily.

"Tell me, why haven't we had one in so long?" asked Oleksandr. "A reunion, I mean. We can't have a get together now. But for the life of me, I can't understand why it has been so long for all of us veterans of the Red Army to get together."

Golubev stared at his friend. "The Revolution?" he said finally.

"Ah. Yes. 'The Fascist Uprising,' as you would say back in the Motherland."

"Well, we're all Fascists now."

"Say hello to your new boss. He's just like your old boss," Oleksandr said with an exhale.

Gulobev nodded. "So, you ended up at the nuclear plant?"

"Forty years," Oleksandr said with a slow nod.

"Beats the army."

"Not always."

Golubev knew what he meant. He was eagar to know more, but didn't know how to broach the subject with his old friend. "Was it like they said?" he asked.

"The 'official' reports? Please. What do you think?" Oleksandr said.

"Standard Empire," Golubev concluded.

"With standard, faulty, half-assed Empire shit."

Golubev paused. "And him?"

"Standard Shevchenko . . ." Oleksandr said, closing his eyes and shaking his head.

A moment passed.

"So, why?" Golubev asked, breaking the silence.

"Because the dead don't talk, Golubev."

"But *you* were there?"

Oleksandr sighed and nodded. "I was there."

"And so?"

"Like I said. We don't talk."

The two men looked at each other, smoking in silence.

"Olek, you're breaking curfew," Golubev said finally.

"Nonsense! Curfew isn't for another thirty minutes!" Oleksandr pointed at his watch in protest.

"No, curfew is now at 9 p.m. To protect against sabotage and conspirators."

"On whose orders?" asked Oleksandr.

"Mine," said Golubev firmly.

Oleksandr didn't respond. He knew he couldn't protest the policy, even if he was talking with an old friend.

"Olek, go home."

Oleksandr nodded slowly. "Good night, Comrade Major," he said, stamping out his cigarette. Walking away from the extinguished lamppost, he disappeared into the night.

From the darkness, Golubev heard Oleksandr's voice.

"Though, you'll always be Comrade Private to me!"

The comment put a smirk on Golubev's face. He looked down and noticed a large smattering of fresh cigarette butts on the ground in front of him.

Switching off his flashlight, he looked up at the sky again, dappled with stars. They shone brightly.

CHAPTER 8

In the rubble and destruction, the fighting is relentless.

Driving East, precious ground is recaptured.

The streets are filled with the burned-out remains of tanks. Abandoned equipment from panicked Invaders is left to rust.

Advancing on lies. Now retreating with truth. And next to it all, the bodies of the fallen.

And then the discoveries. The awful discoveries.

Mass graves. Bodies piled into pits of despair. Hastily covered-up crimes. Mayhem reflecting the madness ordering it.

And the stories from those who bore witness. Door-to-door executions. Tortures. Women of all ages taken to dark cellars for nightly horrors. Children vaporised.

Their stories flow West. The brave. The terrified. The

murdered. Those alive take the call from the graves. They beg for help.

For God's sake, this man cannot stay in power.

But in God's abdication, it is for humanity to decide.

And so, He remains. Destroying from afar. Recommitting to His task. Committing fresh crimes at arm's length. Pressing His remaining advantages with increasing fury.

There is but one tactic. Destruction.

But His fury is one of failure.

Though He lunged for the heart, the Reaper had been denied. Bravery. Honour. The Cause. Home. They don't exist in the papers of certainty. And unlike the best laid plans, these virtues survive the first shot. Then they thrive.

The Capital has been saved. Proud. Free. Her liberty secured thanks to that great unknowable of planned combat: Hope.

Because those who have it can never die.

CHAPTER 9

Across the city, the search was on.

Those involved were to be found, arrested and punished. An example was to be made.

Mikhailovich made it clear that anyone with information leading to the apprehension of the Fascists responsible for this most outrageous offence would be generously rewarded.

Except, as tends to happen, there was no information to speak of. It was an utter mystery what had happened. A miracle, even.

The lead up to Patriots' Day had been unremarkable enough. Nothing suggested that there was to be any trouble whatsoever. Overall, the city continued to move as it needed, and the people went about their duties as directed. Those who weren't Native to the area might have been persuaded to believe that nothing had changed in the behaviour or demeanour of the locals.

As promised by Oksana, the work at the nuclear plant went on without fuss. Absenteeism fell. Children went to school and learned the Mother tongue, or at least pretended to. Businesses functioned within permitted hours of operation, accepting the new currency when it was available. Nobody objected to carrying the Motherland-issued phones. All was well.

Well, sort of.

What was missing was warmth. There were no smiles from the locals for the Invaders. For these interlopers there was to be only a perfunctory professionalism.

Between the locals themselves, however, there was a silent, stoic solidarity. A head tip there. A handshake there. A quick hug when you got the chance. And of course, the whispers. If you knew, you knew.

The list of new Ordinances as decreed by the Motherland, along with their penalties, had gone up on notice boards across the city and were sent out via the Motherland's messenger apps. For the most part, the directives had been duly observed.

The ban on colours matching the Nativist flag was honoured. The forbidden Nativist slogans – "Glory to the Heroes" had been a favourite – were abandoned. Contraband books and documents were turned over. Social media applications, already impossible to use with network blockages, were deleted from Homeland phones anyway. Even the ban on Native music seemed to hold, though what people were listening to through their headphones was largely impossible to determine, even for the military police.

But then there was the Breach.

The Breach was the talk of the town. Except it wasn't, for it was forbidden to discuss what had happened that day under penalty of imprisonment. In the corners of quiet rooms, in comfortable company, people whispered of it. Snickered at it. Admired the ones who carried it out for their audacity, their sheer bravery.

People exchanged knowing nods to one another in the street. It seemed everyone had been there, even those who couldn't have.

And to see it, well, that was to believe it.

In bedrooms across Heryvin, the very idea of the Breach put smiles on faces drifting off to sleep. Older parents thought of it as they worried about their young ones fighting in the East or abroad in the West. Memory of the event was like a warm blanket. Of course, nobody knew who did it or how it was done. Only that it was. And it had been glorious. Heroic. And for anyone who *did* know, it was sure to have been conveniently forgotten.

Who knew a few splashes of children's paint could infuriate an entire Empire?

* * *

"How has class been, Elena?" asked Golubev, removing his cap as usual. "Are the children coping with the, erm, changes?"

Elena shrugged. "Classes are smaller. Without teachers, we've also had to combine cohorts. But we make do, as we can."

She busied herself over paperwork at her desk. The small surface was piled high with student papers, administrative documents, timesheets and class plans, making her seem even more diminutive than usual.

"And the children?" Golubev asked, taking a seat opposite.

Elena looked at him through her glasses without responding. It was the same look she had given countless unruly schoolchildren and would no doubt give to countless more.

The withering stare took effect; Golubev's cheeks began to redden. "Yes, I can imagine it is difficult for them."

"You imagine?" Elena replied, staring through her glasses that now rested on the tip of her nose. "Tell me, Major Golubev, what is it you imagine?"

Golubev shuffled slightly. It was amazing how quickly even grown men could regress to overgrown children in a principal's office.

Regaining his composure, Golubev took out a note pad and pen. "Principal Kovalenko, as you know, there is an investigation underway into the events of Patriots' Day and associated ongoing breaches of the Ordinances."

Elena couldn't help but smile. "And you think the

children were responsible?" she asked, raising her eyebrows. She was enjoying herself now.

"I have been instructed to enquire as to your whereabouts on the day in question."

"Why, I was at the parade and the grand unveiling with everyone else. Where else would I be?"

"And the evening prior?"

"I was at home. As I am every night. Evenings around here have become rather boring, as you might imagine," Elena answered, turning her hands up for effect.

"And who were you with, Principal?"

"Are these questions really all that necessary? If you think I've done something, then feel free to arrest me. Otherwise, I have a lot of work to get on with."

"Elena, please do not make this any more difficult. I assume you were with family, yes?"

She did not respond.

"Yes?" Golubev said again, still looking at his pad.

"I was alone, as a matter of fact."

"And your family?"

"They are dead," Elena snapped.

Golubev looked up. Her eyes were rimmed with red, but no tears fell.

She gathered her composure, hoping her emotions hadn't been noticed.

"I am . . . I am sorry for your loss," Golubev said gently.

His eyes wandered to the shelf above her shoulder, where he noticed a photo of a younger Elena next to a man about her age, along with a teenage boy. A pang of shame swept over him. He felt like a fool for asking such a hurtful question.

"It is not your apology to make. And I do not ask for it," Elena replied, wiping her eyes.

Elena noticed Golubev looking at the picture frame behind her and began to busy herself with nothing in particular. "And so, as I was saying, is there anything else I can help you with, Comrade Major? As I mentioned, we are horribly understaffed, and I don't imagine you are moonlighting as a substitute teacher."

He paused. "Is there anyone who could confirm you were at home, Elena? A neighbour, perhaps?"

"Only my husband and son, but I am not sure they will be much help in your investigation."

His eyes widened in confusion. "I . . . I don't . . ."

"They were killed in the Frontier Wars, if you must know. My darling Vasyl and my little Yuriy died defending our Homeland from your people's bastardy. Gone in honour. Gone forever." Her eyes flamed and she turned and pointed at the photo. "They were gunned down ten years ago *that* day, the day before your godawful Patriots' Day. So, that night, I placed candles out for them under the Icon of Christ in my building. This was all that I could manage to mark their lives, to honour their sacrifice, because of your evil invasion."

She paused to take a breath, and her voice began to rise. "And now? Now the children of this school are my family. And you – you and your kind are killing *them* too. I've seen the footage of destroyed schools, of bombed-out children's hospitals. So please, Major Golubev, why don't you apologise for that? Or better still, apologise to my pupils directly. Apologise for making them orphans, or holding their mothers and fathers hostage in the plant. Apologise for erasing their futures. Apologise for threatening to turn this city into one enormous crater."

Golubev struggled to find the words. "I . . . I . . ."

"Or better yet. Leave me be. It is all I ask."

The two stared at each other, with only the ticking clock filling the silence.

"They died with honour," Golubev said softly.

Elena glanced at him with scepticism. "And what do you know of it?"

"It is, if I may, the one thing that is undeniable in war and death. Every solider, irrespective of his orders or his affiliation, dies with honour – every soldier of honour, that is. Of which, sadly it must be said, there are fewer today."

"And I ask you again, Major Golubev, what do you know of it? Do you know what it is to lose a son? To lose a husband? These might be soldiers to you, but they were my family. They were my everything!"

Golubev shook his head slowly and apologetically. "It

was a lifetime ago. It hardly matters now . . ." Golubev said, trailing off into his own memories.

"It hardly matters? It hardly matters? This is what you sit and tell me?" Elena spat the words as her resolve finally betrayed her and a tear rolled down her cheek. She stood and took the photo from the shelf, shoving it in his face. "You tell *them* it hardly matters."

A wave of guilt washed over Golubev. Guilt for the War. Guilt for Elena's lost son and husband. Guilt for the whole damn, wasteful thing.

After a moment, he began to rise from his chair. "A grieving mother does not need to hear the reflections of a broken-down old soldier. Forgive me, Principal."

For reasons she did not understand, Elena reached across the table and touched him on the arm. As angry as she was, something about this strange man told her to do so. A compassion, perhaps. A shared humanity.

Golubev looked at the small hand touching his sleeve. Though Elena did not look her age, her hands told the truth of her tougher-than-usual life. Just like his own mother, who had suffered immensely under the oppression of the Empire. He looked at Elena, and though he wanted to stay and give her some comfort, he thought better of it. There was no sense aggravating such a deep and unfathomable agony.

Again, he turned to leave, and again, the small hand

pulled at his sleeve. Elena did not say anything. She didn't need to. Her eyes said it all. The eyes of grief.

Golubev sat back into his chair and closed his eyes. "When I was a young soldier," he began, "no older than your Yuriy, I served in the Empire's army as part of the doomed attempts to quell the South Asian uprising. Because my father was an officer stationed in the Western provinces, I enlisted in a division not too far from here. Those of us who enlisted, we fought the Empire's last war under our old colours. It was a war with little rationality, but at least we understood the objective. The preservation of an ideal – one lost long before, perhaps – still made some level of sense to us then. Even if it was a lie, it was a good lie. A worthy lie.

"We were deployed into an area I would not send my worst enemy. Dust and desert. Endless mountains. Oppressive heat. Freezing nights. An invisible opponent. We were boys. And we were scared.

"One particular night, our unit came under heavy fire. We were surrounded. Rescue and air support were impossible, thanks to the advanced Western weapons in the hands of our enemy. Any soldier will tell you, once air superiority is lost, hope is lost. The fighting was some of the fiercest I have ever seen. Men were dying in one another's arms. I had said my goodbyes and made my penance with God."

Elena leaned forward in her chair. She was listening intently now.

"And then, a miracle. Somehow, against orders and odds, a helicopter made it through to our position. An angel from heaven. It sat there in the open, waiting for our extraction, while risking everything. The few of us remaining scrambled and fought our way to it. Somehow, through heavy fire below, we made it back. I still cannot understand how it was possible that we survived. But we did. It was bravery and honour on a level I had never seen before. Or since."

Golubev paused, his eyes staring into the distance before he continued. "After we were returned to our base, the helicopter flew to its division along with the handful of brave rescuers. But the pilot, he stayed with us. Until he was sure we were receiving the medical attention we needed, he simply would not go. Though we would serve more missions together during the war, once we returned home, I did not know what became of this man. A braver man, one could not hope to meet."

He turned to face Elena. "And those who come from such stock, even today, are just as honourable. They will always be so."

Elena was quiet, thinking. "I knew of a pilot who made such a rescue. You speak of Timofei Shevchenko?"

"You knew him?"

"I did. He was my friend. We grew up together. In fact, he was my first kiss." Elena laughed at the memory.

"A handsome hero. You could do worse! I'd have kissed

him too if he'd have had me," Golubev replied, laughing along. He grew quiet as he remembered the man. "I owe him my life. I owe him everything."

"We all do," Elena replied.

"Until I read of The Accident, I did not know what had become of Timofei. The war ended. Life went on." Golubev paused, his face turning to stone. "I read, but I did not believe. This was a man of courage, a man of honour. I knew that no matter what had happened here, Timofei Shevchenko's involvement was that of bravery. I still know it."

"Those of us here, we know the truth of what happened," Elena said. "Perhaps, then, you know another local man who served there alongside Timofei. Oleksandr Abramovich?"

"Ha! I do. Another honourable man. A man of the Union, as I understand, yes?" Golubev replied, his eyes lighting up.

"A *people* of Union," Elena corrected, pointing her finger gently.

Golubev nodded. "Yes, he was there too. Another guardian angel, he came with the helicopter."

"Just like Olek, always on Timofei's coat-tails." Elena smiled before her face shifted to one of concern. "This War is hard on him."

He thought for a moment. "He's a complicated man."

Elena nodded slowly. "After we lost Timofei in The Accident, Olek seemed to lose a small part of himself. He'd followed Timofei to the war. They'd both signed up while

Timofei was studying engineering and Olek was an apprentice. He'd have followed him anywhere. Except . . ." Elena stopped short.

"Yes?" Golubev asked.

She shook her head, freeing herself from the cobwebs of memory. "Now is not the time for old stories, Major Golubev."

"Please, call me Sasha."

Elena smiled. "Will that be all?" she asked.

"It will. Now, Principal Kovalenko, if you do receive information relating to the Fascists and their most recent plot, you will be sure to notify me urgently," Golubev said, placing his hat back on his head.

"Naturally," Elena replied.

He turned to walk away, but not before adding with a shrug, "But of course, some mysteries are just unsolvable."

* * *

"Is this an interrogation or a meeting?" asked Oksana.

Her frustration was finally showing in response to Mikhailovich's persistent questioning. The meeting inside his office had been going for seventy-eight minutes. And Oksana had felt every single one of them.

"Surely you can understand why I would suspect the Union's involvement in such a matter," Mikhailovich replied.

"Oh? And why is that?"

"Unions are notorious hotbeds for political agitators and terrorists."

"Tell me, Lieutenant General, is it the freedom fighting or the free thinking that bothers your kind more?"

He ignored the provocation and continued. "And so, you would have me believe that you, Madam Secretary – the all-powerful Union boss, thou Lady of Golden Lunchboxes – you ask me to take you at your word that you knew *nothing* of what transpired at the unveiling?"

"Once again, I can only tell you I did not. You may choose to believe me, or you may choose to arrest me. Frankly, I am exhausted from keeping this plant of yours operating. I would enjoy a holiday in a different prison, if you were offering it. I do not have time for petulant games or petulant behaviour, as amusing as they may be." Oksana folded her arms and stared at the officer in front of her.

"So, you agree that you were amused!" Mikhailovich barked.

"Your amusement is your own."

Mikhailovich thought back to Patriots' Day. He had been tasked with the unveiling of the new statute of The Commander, which was to be located at the river's mouth between the dam and the nuclear plant. The towering bronze likeness of Mikhailovich's hero would stand as a monument to the Motherland's restoration and The Commander's eternal glory.

The event itself was a great honour for Mikhailovich to host, and the celebration confirmed his professional successes on the battlefield and within the military. Given the importance of the day, he had ensured every detail was personally accounted for. Nothing was left to chance.

And yet somehow, something or *someone* had evaded him. Some crucial detail had slipped through the net. In this moment of supreme triumph, disaster had struck. Sabotage.

To say Mikhailovich did not take his public humiliation well would be an understatement. As far as he was concerned, failure was for mortals. Failure chafed at him like a cheap nylon suit. And yet, there he had stood, in front of the entire city, his failure on display for the world to see. His naked ambition draped in humiliation. It burned.

Thinking back to the events, Mikhailovich could still see it all. His memories were vivid, etched into his brain. The Native music blaring over speakers; the Nativist colours of yellow and blue painted on the bronzed statue; the unsightly flag of barbarians adorning The Commander's likeness as a cape. All of it verboten. All of it utterly, utterly ghastly.

But it was the laughter that haunted him most. The awful, cackling laughter still rang in his ears.

He could still picture the crowds. Those laughing, smug Native faces looking up at him. And Mikhailovich was sure they were *still* laughing. Every day as they walked by him, he could feel their amusement. And who were they to laugh?

Looking at this defiant woman in front of him, he was suddenly incensed anew.

"Miss Shevchenko, you may think that you have leverage here in this relationship of ours. But I assure you, you do not. Yes, I *temporarily* require you and your Union members, but the day will soon come when I do not. It may even be coming sooner than you think. And, rest assured, my memory will be long." He glared at her expressionless face. "The War will be over soon enough. And this pathetic charade of a nation state you call home will be consigned permanently to the underworld of history." Mikhailovich spat as he said the words.

"Wasn't this supposed to be over already?" Oksana asked. "But then, what's a few more days after eight hundred years of oppression?"

Mikhailovich couldn't help but take the bait. "Why is it you do not believe in the historical unity of our two peoples? Surely you know our shared origins and our inherent indivisibility. After all, we are all descendants of the same ancient kingdom founded by the Warrior people, are we not? This trouble between us, this is a family matter. And though we may squabble, like all families do on occasion, we will all come together eventually. Don't you agree?"

Oksana lifted her brows. Now she was the one who couldn't resist engaging with Mikhailovich's taunts. "A *family matter*? Was it a *family matter* when your Great Queen destroyed the beginnings of our young democracy in the eighteenth century?" Oksana asked.

Mikhailovich smiled. "You know your history. Or at least you think you do, Miss Shevchenko. You speak of the Native Horsemen, I assume?" he said.

Oksana did not respond.

"And we sit in their birthplace, do we not? The great Horsemen of the Homeland," Mikhailovich said with faux sincerity.

"We sit in the cradle of democracy, something you might consider looking into," Oksana replied, unable to help herself.

"If you truly knew your history, then you would understand that the Horsemen were true loyalists to the Motherland and the Crown. They were its self-proclaimed protectorate."

"No. They were democratic patriots of a free Homeland."

"Perhaps, once upon a time. But things change; people come to see the light. As you know, it is not how things start but how they finish that matters," Mikhailovich said with a grin. "After all, in the Red Revolution of 1917, it was the Horsemen who pledged their loyalty to the Motherland and the Crown. These supposed heroes of your 'democracy' were nothing more than soldiers of fortune, happy to carry out the whims of the highest bidder or those in charge. And what's more, these pathetic heroes of yours were utter failures in preventing the creation of the Empire, nor could they stop its great expansion West."

Oksana's eyes shot daggers. "All that happened *after* your

Great Queen destroyed their regime and stole our culture as her own hundreds of years earlier. The Motherland co-opted us. And not for the first time."

Mikhailovich rolled his eyes theatrically. While he was growing tired of the Union leader's games, he could at least enjoy the sport of baiting her Nativist sensitivities. "You speak of 1775? Of course, I am no monarchist – I am an Empire man, as you well know – but I will say the Great Queen was right to prevent the dangerous creep of Western, liberal propaganda towards the Motherland. For centuries, previous regimes did likewise. Such dangerous movements on the periphery of the Motherland must be snuffed out, lest they catch on. Every so often, one needs to do a little weeding in the garden. Just as we are now."

"And with such incredible success, Lieutenant General."

"Despite all evidence to the contrary, you still believe that your pathetic Fascist lot can somehow prevail. I only wish I had your futile confidence."

Oksana sighed in frustration and looked away.

Mikhailovich glared at her. "I have no idea where you can draw such belief. You know what is obvious from history, Miss Shevchenko? Seventeen seventy-five, 1917, even in 1921 during your weak resistance of the Empire's early years of expansion – what's clear to any student is that despite your supposedly fierce reputations, those drawn from this region have a very, very long history of losing. And this, Miss Shevchenko, this is one Nativist tradition I will be very happy to see continued!" He smirked with smug satisfaction.

Oksana stared ahead, avoiding Mikhailovich and his obnoxious face.

He was beginning to enjoy himself now. It was time to twist the knife. "Your father was a famous soldier, was he not? Or was he just a failed engineer?"

"Do not speak of my father," Oksana snapped, turning back to face Mikhailovich.

"He too was involved in a failed military campaign, no?"

"A failed war from your failed Empire," Oksana replied, locking eyes with Mikhailovich.

"What is it they say about sending a Horseman to do a Warrior's job?"

Oksana rolled her eyes.

"Never mind. Though had your father been of true Horseman stock, well, he'd have taken the name of a colour or an animal, as those from this area traditionally do," Mikhailovich continued.

"Luckily for me, our name means *cobbler*. But of course, you knew that."

He grinned. Even though he couldn't stand the woman, Mikhailovich couldn't help but be impressed by her clear intelligence. She was a worthy opponent.

"But your name, Miss Shevchenko, goes back well beyond your father – as I'm sure you well know. It makes sense you are a Unionist, given your dissident bloodlines. Or is this a coincidence?"

"I don't know; you're the one giving the history lessons."

Mikhailovich smiled. "Your father's reputation in this city must be a burden for you, no?"

"My father was a great man," Oksana replied, her jaw stiffening slightly.

Suddenly, Mikhailovich barked with an almost maniacal laugh. "Well, perhaps you can succeed where he failed. You can finish his life's work. Afterall, it was Timofei Shevchenko who nearly destroyed this city and large swathes of the Empire's agricultural capacity with his dangerous ineptitude. Can you imagine the humiliation this caused the Empire? To admit our scientists could be so inept?"

"A convenient narrative to cover for a failed, bankrupt system. Anyone who lives here knows what happened. Your kind can try to bury the truth, but you can't destroy it."

"I can only go with the recorded history, I'm afraid," the officer mused as he motioned to his files. "I wonder, did your father do it deliberately?" He reached for a file sitting atop the others and opened it. "I must say, part of me hopes he did it in service of some kind of nefarious plot. Better to be an efficient terrorist than an idiot, wouldn't you agree?"

Oksana stared at him, cold steel in her eyes.

"Ah! Here we are." Mikhailovich picked up a sheet and began to read. "'Timofei Shevchenko, deceased.

"'It is the opinion of this Investigative Committee that Comrade Shevchenko be posthumously censured for his gross negligence and central role' – oh dear, *central* role – 'in the tragic events at Provincial Nuclear Facility 12. As the supervising engineer, Comrade Shevchenko failed to adequately monitor key performance indicators of the plant's nuclear core, did not follow critical protocols, failed to appropriately oversee vital equipment updates and maintenance schedules, and did not provide direction and oversight to the staff in his care when such diligence was vital.

"'Once it was clear PNF12 was in danger of a major meltdown event, Comrade Shevchenko failed to notify senior command of the events transpiring, failed to raise the alarm with international oversight bodies and failed to initiate critical fail-safe protocols that could have prevented this calamity. These were all matters in which he was trained and regularly instructed to obey.

"'It is the unequivocal opinion of this Committee that Comrade Shevchenko is directly responsible for the partial core meltdown that occurred at PNF12, an event that caused the tragic deaths of thirty-one of his colleagues, associated environmental degradation of the surrounding area and international embarrassment for the Empire's nuclear program.

"'Notwithstanding his *rogue* behaviour, Comrade Shevchenko's failures and ineptitude thankfully did not result in what may have been catastrophic event of global proportions. Given these facts, a further review of the Empire's nuclear program or an audit of other nuclear plants in operation is deemed not to be required. The program is, and remains, world leading in its field. The Empire and the Party's Standing Committee are to be commended for their outstanding leadership and attention to detail in these matters.'"

Mikhailovich snapped the file shut. "No, it seems he was just an idiot. How sad."

Oksana's jaw stiffened again.

After staring at her for a few seconds, Mikhailovich shook his head in tedium. "That will be all, Madam Cobbler." He glared as he waved her to the door.

Oksana slowly stood to her feet. She was utterly exhausted.

"Take care, Miss Shevchenko. Take very good care, while you still can."

"You should too, Comrade Lieutenant General. As I understand it, the life expectancy of the Motherland's generals isn't what it once was. Especially the amusing ones." She grinned, suddenly finding new reserves of strength.

His nostrils flared. "Know this, Miss Shevchenko: the Fascists responsible for this crime will be found. And if I have it my way, they will hang."

"Hanging Fascists. We can only hope . . ." Oksana replied as she walked from the room.

As the door closed, Mikhailovich sat alone. He turned his chair and looked out the window.

Pouring himself a drink, his mind turned back once again to the events of Patriots' Day. But he would find those responsible. And they would pay. The thought gave him comfort, and he smiled slightly to himself.

Drinking whisky in the darkness, Mikhailovich wondered what those back East thought of it all. But if they were laughing, they wouldn't be for much longer.

CHAPTER 10

In the East, the Invasion was proceeding as planned.

It had always been planned this way, to focus on the East and the South and to ignore the Capital. To nibble rather than devour. Besides, the heart could be destroyed without being captured.

Most importantly, there were no errors. How could there be? This was a perfectly executed plan.

And anyone who suggested otherwise was a Collaborator. An enemy of the Motherland. A fifth column to be hunted in hearts and minds. And feverish dreams.

Everyone agreed with the objects of the Special Operation. Especially those who couldn't get out without leaving anyone behind. Those people believed the hardest.

Western economic sanctions against the regime were

being tightened. But they could happily be ignored. The Motherland was impervious.

In the West, the heroin of cheap energy was needed.

The Commander knew what this meant: the veins and pipelines would not close. A carefully cultivated addiction meant the money would keep flowing East. Killing had never been so profitable.

Foreign businesses, always suspect, had been ejected without their hoped-for Eastern riches. They would be replaced and improved! The Motherland would provide for her people!

In the West, waverers could be reliably picked off with empty promises.

Corrupted sand was thrown in the gears. Unity could be compromised, as it always had been. Chipped away at. Eroded. Facts were explained away. So were the crimes.

Hopeful and more convenient truths were peddled along with alternative histories. So-called bigger pictures were advocated by those with small minds and even smaller hearts.

Peace. Who doesn't want peace? Surely, we can at least talk. What harm could come from that?

Who would blink first?

Granaries were robbed. Ports were blockaded. It was time to share the pain. And the butchery. The world could starve if it dared imposed sanctions.

Election season. Narrow majorities. Gas and groceries.

Kitchen-table issues. Global shortages. Escalation risks. Hip pocket nerves. Off-ramps.

When will this end?

How can it end?

How much more can they expect?

Surely they can see how hard it is for us here?

Help is not endless. Or without condition. Surely they can at least see that?

And, besides, nobody wants this to end in His humiliation. We must respect His dignity.

And so, the butchery remains financed. Those in the West paying to watch a made-for-TV genocide in the East.

But even in perfection, there is always room for improvement. The Special Operation could be even more special.

These improvements required replacement in the leadership. Fresh blood to draw more blood. A return to an old playbook of success. Scorch the earth. Make them understand. Make them pay. Break them.

But, despite everything, war's essential truth still peeks through the clouds.

Facts are persistent. They cannot be spun.

Piled-up bodies. Lost limbs. Sons and daughters not returning home. Generals vaporised daily. Ancient capitals not yet conquered. Battles lost. Days becoming weeks. Weeks becoming months. A grinding blitzkrieg.

Facts.

In the South, the heroes gather for their shot.

Bombardment from the ocean must be returned. The opportunity comes. A puncher's chance is taken. An incredible success creates a more incredible humiliation.

The Motherland's mothership is returned to her maker.

David has hurt Goliath.

In the East, this could not be hidden. While in the West, it was seen by those who wished to look away.

CHAPTER 11

THE BELLS RANG, signalling the end of the school day.

With classes finishing later in the day, the sun hung low in the sky. For many parents, long hours were expected across the city due to worker shortages, so the school tried to fill the gap in adult supervision. The longer hours put pressure on teachers, but Elena didn't mind if it meant giving parents a break. She knew they needed it.

She walked the halls, saying goodbye to children and greeting parents on pick-up duty. Exhausted faces and vacant eyes greeted her, but they still smiled at her warmly.

School 50, though usually a primary school, had been combined with the local high school to create one point of teaching for the city. With the school now servicing children of all ages, this meant mixed classroom learning for the teachers and more self-directed time for older students.

"Self-directed teens, what will they think of next? Self-walking dogs?" a teacher named Tanya had said to Elena when she first suggested the approach at a staff meeting.

Elena had tried to defend the idea, but she knew Tanya was right. But what else could be done? Though she and her teachers were doing their best, Elena felt terrible for the disrupted education of the young minds in her care.

First, it had been the virus. And now this.

"Kids are resilient," teachers would repeat in the lunchroom to reassure one another. But Elena worried how they would ever catch up for all this lost learning, if at all. And what about the scars from this horrific War? What would that do to warp these young minds as they grew closer to adulthood?

It was a terrible time to be a young person. It was all so unfair for young souls with their futures still ahead of them. And yet Elena knew if they were only a little bit older, they would be fighting and dying on the battlefield. It was all too awful to contemplate. And yet it was real.

These worries filled her mind as she turned the corner in the school corridor. Up ahead, she saw three senior girls standing near a locker. They quickly broke apart once they saw Elena coming, the universal tell for being up to no good.

"Katya, Irina, Masha, what are you girls up to?" Elena asked.

"Nothing, Principal Kovalenko," said Katya, the tallest of

the three girls. Trying to look casually innocent, Katya began to pull up her long dark brown hair into a ponytail.

"And Masha, Irina? You're also up to nothing?" Elena stared at them over the top of her glasses. She knew Masha and Irina well. Unlike Katya, they were not used to challenging authority or standing up to a cross-examination from the principal.

Though she was smiling with her teeth, Katya was shooting eye daggers at Masha and Irina. Like Elena, Katya knew who the weak links were too. "Honestly, Principal Kovalenko, we were just talking about a boy Irina is going on a date with this weekend. Isn't that right, *Irina*?"

"Oh, yes, that's right. Yes, we're going to a movie," Irina blurted out.

"A movie? Is that so?" Elena said.

"Well, not a *movie* movie, right, Irina? Netflix," Katya said, knowing full well the cinemas had been shut since the War began. Her accomplices were utter idiots.

Elena raised an eyebrow. "Netflix? That's funny. I haven't been able to watch Netflix since the beginning of the invasion. I thought it had been blocked here by the new servers. Perhaps you girls could show me how to log in on my phone? I'm sure it's my fault. I'm so hopeless with all this technology." She took out her phone and offered it to the girls.

"Not *Netflix* Netflix," Katya said, her voice sweetening. "You know what I mean. A movie at home. That's how we date now. No drive-ins anymore," she laughed awkwardly.

"Oh, of course, that makes sense," Elena said, taking her phone back. "And tell me, Irina, who is this lucky young man joining you for the big event?"

"Erm, well, it's Andrei," Irina squeaked with very little certainty.

"Andrei Mironov? Why, I thought he was going out with your friend Vikka."

While the conversation was underway, Masha was fiddling with something in the pockets of her skirt.

"Out with it," Elena said sternly, holding out her hand with the palm facing upwards.

Masha looked at Katya for support.

"Now!" said Elena.

It was clear to the girls that Elena was no longer playing around. Slowly, Masha took her hand of her pocket. The game was up.

Katya closed her eyes and sighed as Masha deposited the object into Elena's outstretched palm. Defeated and embarrassed, Masha dropped her head.

The feel of warm, heavy metal in her palm surprised Elena. She had been anticipating cigarettes. Or worse. She looked down at the postage-stamp-sized flag pin in her hand. The polished yellow and blue metal gleamed.

Elena's breath caught in her throat. "Girls . . ." she said, trailing off. She realised then she hadn't see her Native flag in weeks.

"I can explain. We thought—" Masha started.

Though touched, the principal was seized by another emotion: fear for these young, brave souls. "Masha, that will be enough!"

Masha happily stopped speaking. She knew how terrifying Principal Kovalenko could be in such moments.

Elena closed her hand tightly over the contraband. "Do you girls understand what sort of trouble you can get into for carrying an item like this?"

Masha's and Irina's heads both dropped. They knew the trouble they were in. Katya looked ahead, her eyes burning with resentment. What were they being accused of, Katya thought. Loving their country?

"Carrying the Native flag – even *wearing* the colours in combination – is now punishable by prison. *Prison*, girls. And you three are of criminal age now. There can be no excuse for this sort of behaviour."

Elena then turned to face Irina, palm outstretched. "Yours too, please."

Irina quickly handed over her object without fuss. She was glad to be rid of it. She wished she hadn't listened to Katya and her stupid idea.

"Katya," Elena said, motioning for the girl to fork over her pin. Katya rolled her eyes before digging into her pocket. She slapped the metal into Elena's hand, causing it to clink loudly against the other two.

"And how many of these are there?" Elena said, looking at Katya.

"That is what we have. Only you have them now."

"And if I were to look inside your locker? What would I find there?"

Katya did not respond.

Elena studied the girls. "Irina, Masha, I would like some time with Katya, please. You will both be in to see me first thing tomorrow. Understood?"

They both nodded without looking up.

"Go home," Elena said. Before the girls could respond, she spoke again, only with a louder voice. "Straight home!"

Masha and Irina didn't require a second order. Irina was already down the hallway before Masha gave a small, apologetic glance to a seething Katya. Masha turned and briskly jogged to catch up to her friend.

Elena looked at Katya and waited until the other two were out of earshot. She nodded to the locker. "Open it," she said.

"But, I . . ." Katya said.

"Open. It." Elena was in no mood for this dangerous game.

The girl's shoulders fell as she sighed. She reached out a hand to her tall, grey locker and spun the code. The door swung open.

Inside, next to several textbooks and a pair of Nike

sneakers, was an enormous plastic bag of Native flag pins, probably in the hundreds.

"Katya! Have you lost yourself?" Elena said, slamming the locker door shut. Elena's face had turned from stern, parental anger to genuine concern. "Where did you get these?"

"It doesn't matter," Katya replied, turning her body away to face the locker door.

Elena spun Katya around and held her gently by the shoulders. Though the girl was much taller and longer limbed than Elena, her teen slouch ensured they were both eye to eye. "My girl, this is not a game," she said, looking into Katya's fierce blue eyes. "You must tell me. You must. Who gave you these?"

"I don't know the person. There are things left on the edge of the city every night. Things for us to find. Things from those who are still fighting."

"My child, you mustn't take or carry these things! The danger you have put yourself and your friends in, you have no idea!"

"What danger? We don't fight. We sit here, reading books. We sit here while people die. There *is* no danger here."

"There is danger everywhere!" Elena exclaimed. "It lurks around every corner. Just because you can't see it doesn't mean you are safe. You have no idea how far the enemy sees and reaches. Not everyone can be trusted, my dear girl."

"Nobody saw me," Katya said.

"How do you know?"

The girl paused. "I . . ."

"There are spies *everywhere*, my dear," Elena said. "Now, how is it you are getting these things? How did you know where to find these in the first place? Tell me you are not using messaging services."

"No, I would never use their phones like that. We aren't *idiots*, Principal. You forget, you might be older, but we grew up with these things. No, outside the city, if you find the right places, our old phones – they work. We've known about this, but we don't tell anyone. But if you know, you know. The Heroes are placing SkyLinks to connect us where they can. It doesn't always work, but you can get messages. And then there are drops of things like this."

Elena's eyes widened. "My child, this is not a game. This is life and death, with serious consequences. And what of your grandfather?"

"Please don't tell Papa Olek!" Katya said, her youth suddenly breaking her tough exterior.

"Surely you know the Union is already suspected of responsibility for the incident on Patriots' Day."

Katya dropped her head.

"Had you been caught with this," Elena said, holding up one of the flag pins, "they'd have assumed it was from Papa Olek. And then he'd have been arrested. Or worse."

"I know Papa Olek says we mustn't fight. But I don't

believe him." Katya felt the tears welling in her eyes. "I don't want to believe him. I don't understand how he can sit and watch what is happening to us. I just wanted to help. To give people hope. I wanted them to know that they – that we – still exist, even it this small, tiny way. It was so each of us could have something to hold on to, you know?" She looked up at Elena. "I feel so useless. I hear the stories from those fighting. And then I hear what's happening where the Invaders are. I hear what they do to us, especially the girls . . ." she said, her eyes returning to the floor. "And I want them to pay."

Elena's breath caught in her throat. She'd heard of those horrors too. In a way, she couldn't blame the girl for wanting to strike first. "Your brothers, they are off fighting?"

"Yes, though I haven't heard from them. But I know they're alive! I know they are killing these Invading bastards by the dozens. They're too tough and too smart for them."

"So it's just you and your grandfather?"

The girl nodded slowly.

Elena's heart went out to the girl. She squeezed her shoulders. "Katya, I need you to listen to me," she began in a hushed tone. "I understand how you feel, I do. You are a good girl. You are a proud Native of the Homeland. But there is no use having you die in vain, carrying around trinkets of no consequence. Your time will come. The time to stand up will come, I promise. But not now."

Katya nodded.

"Tell me you understand me. I must hear you say it."

"I understand," Katya said.

"You must trust me. Virtue is on our side. And we will be free again, someday soon. The moment, it will come. And when it does I will be there with you, side by side. I will stand with you. But until that day comes, you must wait, my sweet girl. You must wait."

She opened her arms, and Katya hugged her tightly. It was the first time the teen had hugged anyone since the War began and her brothers left to fight in the East.

"Now, leave those pins there; I will deal with them. But you get home. And I mean *straight* home!" Elena said.

"Yes, Principal," Katya said before turning and scurrying out.

Watching Katya run out the door Elena sighed to herself.

Kids.

CHAPTER 12

The War reverts to the East. Back to where it began when the Frontier Wars started.

The horrors localised. But with intensity. A grinding phase. Of bone and flesh.

In cities where Invaders were repelled, relief turns to sadness.

Courageous women and men head off East.

Heroes come home in caskets.

A conveyor belt of violence.

Burials in churches.

Tears.

A last stand inside a steel works. A dead city bombarded relentlessly.

A horrific lightshow. Nobody can watch. Or look away.

How are they surviving? What is left? Who is left?

And where are they taking the prisoners?

Heroes disappearing. Children taken.

Prison cells await.

And caskets.

Tears.

PART TWO

WINTER

CHAPTER 13

The winter came late but hard, freezing the conflict along existing battlelines for the time being. Blizzards of thick, heavy snow covered the city and the surrounding landscape. With few people coming in or going out, the city began to feel like an isolated fortress detached from the rest of the world.

Despite the oppression, both from weather and the Occupation, the work went on as it usually did during these dreary months.

Winters in the Homeland were never easy. But this season, there was a different kind of hardness etched into the faces around town. If you were not one of those faces, or of them, it was deeply unnerving.

Sokolov watched the sunrise from inside his small private office. From his vantage point above the city, he could see directly onto the town square and farther out to the horizon. Snow ploughs were already clearing the fresh, overnight falls to make way for the day's work.

Sipping coffee, with his long, thin fingers cupping the mug, he thought about how the heavy snow made him feel more isolated, more alone from the world. It was something he felt every winter, but the circumstances of the Occupation made the feeling even more powerful. If he was honest, at times he felt surrounded.

Outside in the freshly scraped square, the usual crowd of locals assembled to take in the coming of the new day.

To Sokolov's puzzled bemusement, the numbers attending had been growing steadily each morning. Today, the attendance was so large that Sokolov could see people spilling into side streets and beyond. It was as though the entire town was turning out now for some kind of must-see event.

Word was clearly spreading. But why?

The sun was so weak at this time of year that, beyond a dull glimmer of light, it could barely be seen at all. It was hardly a visual extravaganza or the stuff of romance, Sokolov thought. Which really made it all the more peculiar.

Having watched the gathering repeatedly, Sokolov knew that for the rest of the day the streets would be deserted. People were staying indoors, away from the frigid cold, unless absolutely necessary.

And yet, this.

It made no sense.

A sentry had notified Sokolov of this peculiar event a fortnight ago. From then on, Sokolov had started observing it but had gotten no closer to the truth of what these people were up to. They were up to something, Sokolov knew that much.

But what did it mean? And how long had it been going on? The Colonel was stumped.

At first the idea of crowds assembling in the city had made him nervous. His first instinct, the instinct of the Occupier, was to send in guards to break it up. He also feared how Mikhailovich might react once he became aware.

But the old intelligence officer in Sokolov said otherwise. For some reason, this event had stirred something inside of Sokolov that had been dormant for years. There was a truth to be understood here, and he wanted to get to the bottom of it.

He had lost the passion for his desk job many years ago. He couldn't remember when it started – who does? – but he also couldn't quite remember when he *didn't* feel this way.

Had it not been for the money, Sokolov wouldn't have signed on to this Special Operation. A career man, he was no ideologue. Certainly not in this modern world. Perhaps, as a young intelligence officer stationed in the West, he had believed for a time. But the Empire? That was a long time ago.

For men like Sokolov, it was easy to be cynical today; he'd seen far too much to believe in any one thing. Or man. It was a "get what you can and get out" world these days, and

Sokolov was fine with that. Unlike some of the young fools around him, he had no intention of dying in this godforsaken place. Not for The Commander, not for the Motherland, not for anyone.

To Sokolov's knowledge, there was no historic precedent or local custom underpinning this peculiar morning ritual. Despite scouring local information sources, he could find no record of sunrise observances in pre-Empire Nativist records. And though he wasn't a theologian, the lack of overt ceremony or observable prayer made a religious event appear unlikely.

It was bizarre.

Earlier that week, Sokolov had gone along to one of these morning events, hoping to find information that might explain what was happening. Under cover of disguise, he stood with the people and listened keenly. But beyond the perfunctory morning chit-chat amongst neighbours, there was nothing of value. According to his observations, there was no central authority or leadership figure present. No organisational principles were evident. No speeches were given. No hymns sung. No chants or slogans. Just a sunrise and a peaceful return home.

Was it a code? Perhaps, but there didn't appear to be one. Nothing was left behind by participants.

Perhaps an opportunity to move goods or product amongst the resisters? Sokolov's agency-trained eyes could not detect anything being exchanged between those present.

Could it be a deliberate distraction? He had his men

posted all over the city just in case an attack came, which of course it didn't.

Sokolov had kept meticulous notes of the number of attendees as well as the names of those who arrived. Though informants were difficult to come by within the tight-knit Nativist community, the newly created city records with experimental facial recognition software made this practice easy enough.

The small physical footprint of the city and its reduced wartime population also helped to keep tabs. Over time, Sokolov began to recognise these faces on his own without any assistance from his records. He'd started the digital surveillance and record keeping before he had been asked, as it had seemed prudent. But in truth, he preferred the old-school methods of his youth. As an agency man, Sokolov believed his eyes saw things that machines couldn't.

However, given that he knew what to expect from Mikhailovich, Sokolov preferred to be on top of potentially trivial matters such as this, rather than have the young leader rant and rave about it later.

Over the course of his long career, Sokolov had seen Mikhailovich's kind before. Brash, confident, assured. Unburdened by what they did not know. And Sokolov knew how to manage them. Managing up was an art, and the ambitious were the easiest of all to manage. You see them coming. Once he knew what these men wanted, he could direct their course more easily. Basic, really.

Fortunately for him, Mikhailovich was straight from this school. An easy mark.

He turned to look out the window, another day, another crowd gathering. But what did it mean?

* * *

Inside Mikhailovich's office, the evening poker game had been going for some time. Outside, the white snow fell heavily onto a quiet, subdued city. Even with a raging fireplace, the cold had forced the three officers to wear heavy coats indoors.

"Careful, or I'll take those comfy quarters of yours soon, Comrade Lieutenant General," said Sokolov, laughing at his luck as he set down his cards. A straight flush.

Looking down at Sokolov's winning hand, Golubev threw away his cards in disgust. "Your luck is either about to run out, or is a product of deceit," he said, taking a sip of his whisky.

"You know, it is bad practice to let the boss lose, Comrade Colonel," said Mikhailovich flatly.

"A hanging offence in the old days of the Empire!" said Sokolov, greedily sweeping the mess of notes and coins toward himself.

"Ah, the good old days . . ." said Mikhailovich.

"Perhaps," said Sokolov as he stacked his winnings into neat piles.

"I wish I had seen it," said Mikhailovich quietly.

Sokolov began to shuffle the deck of cards in preparation of the next poker hand. "Seen what?"

"The Empire," Mikhailovich said, taking a drink from his glass.

Golubev shrugged. "It was what it was."

"I was born in it, but I have no memory of it. It is the most frustrating thing to me," said Mikhailovich. "I envy you both." He toasted his glass ever so slightly to his companions before bringing it to his mouth.

Sokolov couldn't help but laugh. "You are too young to be envious," he said, dealing the cards.

"Can you imagine?" Mikhailovich continued. "The world's greatest ideological triumph: the Motherland. Ascendant. Respected. A time of serious men, of serious challenge. A time of titans and great power politics!"

"With serious problems," Golubev said, picking up the cards dealt to him.

Mikhailovich paused on the comment, thinking to himself. He left the pile in front of him untouched as he watched Golubev and Sokolov reorder their cards. "You don't think much of our Empire, do you, Comrade Major?"

"It is not that I don't think much of it, Lieutenant General. I simply don't think of it," Golubev replied. "I lived it. I have seen both sides of history. One learns not to be sentimental."

"Yes, quite," Mikhailovich said. "But both sides are not coequal, you might agree?"

"There were positives and negatives in both, that's true. But that's life, is it not? There is, I'm afraid, no perfection. That is what the rulers of the Empire came to realise. Those in charge saw the perfection of the promise had permanently eluded them." He watched Sokolov turn the house cards over.

"Perhaps they needed more time or perseverance?" Mikhailovich asked.

"Perhaps," Golubev said noncommittedly. Having seen the cards on the table, he placed a bet without looking at his cards again, or at either man.

Sokolov grunted his agreement with Golubev before looking at his cards and placing down a bet of his own. "Raise," he said confidently.

"But surely you agree that the Empire was globally respected?" Mikhailovich said, noticing he was suddenly outnumbered by the older men.

Golubev, watching Sokolov intently, matched the bet. "It is not merely a question of respect. What is respect, if it is not centred in reality? You need to match words with capability." He looked back at his own cards with slight puzzlement.

"Do you want to know my first memory?" the young officer said, the comment directed to neither man. "I was at home. I was a small boy, not yet of school age. It was the summertime, and I was playing outside with my brothers. Our father came home from work. He was a stern man, a serious man. Thanks to thieves and collaborators – those let in after the Empire's Wall came down – the local auto plant was being closed. Having dedicated himself to producing the people's automobiles, my father was now out of work, just like every other man in town. Now, of course, being a proud and good man, my father set off looking for work so that he could provide for us. He promised to return for us all, once he found it."

The poker bet had turned to Mikhailovich, who was no longer paying attention, so the card game stopped. Not daring to prompt their superior, both Sokolov and Golubev listened with a detached bemusement as he continued.

"My mother cried and cried. She begged my father not to go as he pushed her aside and walked out the door, a small bag in hands. How she pleaded! My brothers, well, they believed my father would come back for us. He was a man of his word, they said. But somehow, I knew. I knew from that moment on, I would never see him again. And so I would hug my mother as she cried herself to sleep every night. It was all I could do. I hugged her when the men who . . . 'visited' her left too.

"In my childhood, I saw what happens when the decadent and the depraved capture a nation. I know what happens when a nation loses – or a family loses – respect from others and for itself. Tell me, have either of you ever had to beg neighbours for food? Have you watched your mother prostitute herself to the fat, filthy pig fathers of your classmates? Have you felt the scorn of their mothers and betrayed wives, as though it were somehow your fault?

"Like our country, I felt the mockery of strangers. The inability to provide for oneself. The need to rely on others, on those who would seek to exploit what little you have and then constantly remind of that trade. They say pride is sinful. But to have none, well, that is pathetic.

"But we are no longer pathetic. And they certainly respect us now . . ." Mikhailovich trailed away, taking a long sip of his whisky before continuing on. "Thankfully, The Commander cleared it all up. He ended the madness. He made us whole." His thoughts concluded, he pretended to look at his cards with sudden vigour.

"They do respect us, sir," said Sokolov, looking at Golubev with some hesitation.

Mikhailovich nodded slowly. "Yes. Though it must be said, not all. But in time they will too."

Sensing danger ahead, Sokolov attempted to shift the conversation elsewhere. "Of course. Of course, how right you are! Now, how are you betting here, Comrade Lieutenant General? It sits with you. Something tells me your luck is about to change."

Ignoring Sokolov, Mikhailovich was now standing. He looked out the window and into the distance, tapping the now-collapsed fan of cards against his teeth. "And what of this 'sunrise' nonsense?" Mikhailovich said, finally breaking the silence.

"Ah, yes, I have observed this. There is not much to know,

it would appear," Sokolov said, pretending to be disinterested in the topic.

"But it is daily, is it not? What do you make of it, Colonel? You must have a theory, no?"

"Native culture is primitive and backward. It is, perhaps, some sort of regional observance for these savages of which we have no prior record or knowledge."

"Perhaps? This is what you bring me? Idle speculation?"

"I bring you what I have, sir. Names, records, patterns." Sokolov set down his cards and sparked up a cigarette. He exhaled loudly after filling his lungs with smoke.

"Given you asked for my speculation, I provide it. But I do not tender it as fact."

"It feels like some secret of which we are not a part. You can understand how it exercises the mind, Colonel," said Mikhailovich

"I can, sir. But I have looked at this for several weeks now, and I am confident it can be dismissed as a mere peculiarity of the locals."

Mikhailovich was unconvinced. But stroking his chin, he was unable to offer any competing alternative proposition himself.

"It's the flag," said Golubev.

The other two men looked at him. Mikhailovich appeared most intrigued.

"They are simulating a Nativist flag-raising ceremony," Golubev said.

"I'm sorry, I do not understand your point, Comrade Major," Sokolov said.

"Comrade Colonel, tell me, have your sentries been observing the sunsets to monitor for crowds?" Golubev continued.

"Naturally," Sokolov said.

"And? Nobody. Am I right?" Golubev said with a degree of excitement.

Sokolov smirked. The bastard had a point.

"You see! Look, here! It is a rising sun. A yellow sun rising into the blue sky. The image is clear. A blue horizontal stripe sitting above a yellow one. Sky, sun." Golubev pulled his phone from his pocket, showing the Native flag on its screen to both men to underscore his point.

"Perhaps, perhaps," Sokolov said, stubbing his cigarette into a nearby ashtray.

Golubev grinned with triumph.

"Ah, you know it to be true! Mister KSU. Mister Mystery. Outfoxed at his own game of intrigue by old, broken-down Sasha," Golubev said, pointing his finger playfully.

Sokolov could not help but chuckle. As a theory, it made sense. While he was frustrated he didn't uncover this mystery himself, the sheer relief from the agonising riddle gave him comfort. But Sokolov wasn't ready to give into his old friend just yet.

"But you'd agree this is a most obscure reference. If it was true, who is it in service of?" Sokolov said, playing along.

"It is akin to a Nativist sacrament," Golubev said, warming to his thesis. "Think about it. They currently have no way of displaying their Nativist identification. No colours, language, artefacts are permitted per the Ordinances, which we are brutally enforcing. This 'sunrise' ritual, well, it is a way for them to be connected to their history and identification. And what's more, they can do so in full sight, without hindrance from any of us. It's quite clever when you think about it."

Sokolov laughed. "As far as Nativists plots go, it is perhaps the cleverest of all!"

The sudden loud smash of glass splintered the conversation.

Startled, Golubev and Sokolov instinctively reached for their pistols while jumping to attention. Within seconds, they understood what had happened.

Mikhailovich stood hunched over his desk with his back to them. Whisky and glass shards ran down the far wall of the office.

Golubev looked at Sokolov from the corner of his eye. Though he pretended not to notice, Golubev registered the look of concern on Sokolov's face.

"This mockery, this endless mockery. It cannot stand," Mikhailovich muttered to himself as he began pacing the room.

"Let it go, Comrade Lieutenant General. It is meaningless. It is designed to infuriate. You must not let it," Sokolov said, trying to placate his boss to little effect.

"What I must do – what I must *have* – is disciplined order in this city. This is what must occur." He stopped pacing to look out the window of his office into the darkness.

"They seek to unnerve you," Sokolov said.

"It is *they* who shall be unnerved!" Mikhailovich said with a dark fury.

Silence hung in the room. Sokolov and Golubev knew there was nothing more to be said.

The game was over.

* * *

Sokolov was smoking outside the building archway. He held his left hand out to catch some of the falling snow before dusting it off against his tailored jacket. In moments like this, he could cut an almost regal figure.

Suddenly, Golubev shoved Sokolov from behind. Hard.

Sokolov staggered forward into the heavy snow, nearly tumbling to the ground in the process. After gathering his footing, he turned sharply to see who had the nerve to push a senior military officer in that fashion.

"You absolute fool. I could have you court marshalled for that!" While he would never admit it, the sight of Golubev immediately lowered Sokolov's fight-or-flight instincts, which, thanks to the push, had been placed on high alert.

"Go ahead. It wouldn't be the first time," said Golubev.

Sokolov picked up his cigarette from the snow-covered ground, inspected it from both ends, and put it back in his mouth. He contemplated Golubev in front of him, who was clearly agitated. "Jesus, Sasha, what's gotten into you?" He took a deep drag on his cigarette.

"What's got into me? Please. I am the only sane man in an asylum."

"Ah, yes, I had missed your martyrdom." Sokolov blew a puff of smoke into the air.

"Sok, this is getting out of hand."

"What is?"

Golubev gestured upwards to the Administration building. "This. The War. The situation in this city. *Him.*"

"Be careful in your tone, Major."

"Don't give me this rank nonsense, Sok. He's not here."

The Colonel took another drag on his cigarette. He understood what his old friend was thinking. The same had been troubling him for some time.

"And what do you imagine happens?" Sokolov said, exhaling.

"What do you mean?"

"Well, play it out for me. How does it happen? We resist the orders. Then we go home. Nobody is the wiser. Life goes on. Is that it?"

Golubev let out a soulless chuckle. "Spare me your simplicity. It is not resisting orders. It is simply making sure this doesn't descend into madness. Beyond what it already has, that is."

"It's fine. He is a child with toys, a boy pretending to be a man. Harmless," Sokolov said with a shrug, trying to reassure himself as much as Golubev.

"You know full well he is not harmless. It's unsettling. And, what's more, you indulge his worst instincts. That is not the role of a senior officer. Your role is to provide the advice our leaders must hear. Instead, you pander. Why, I have no idea."

"I told him he mustn't let the Nativists and Fascists get under his skin," Sokolov replied. "What else would you have me do, *Alexander*?"

Golubev rolled his eyes. He couldn't remember the last time his friend had called him by his full given name. "You know full well how you are with him. I am asking you to stop. For all our sakes."

Sokolov snorted and continued to smoke.

"When did you get so cynical?" Golubev asked.

"When I stopped listening to you. Do you ever wonder why you never get promoted? You could learn a little pandering."

"I know you were always a little this way, what with your intelligence training at the KSU. But this, this is worse. In the past, you'd have handled a ranking officer like this the right way. You wouldn't just let him off the leash."

"I think you're imagining a different man," Sokolov replied.

Golubev shook his head. "Maybe I am."

"Your problem, Sasha, is that you believe you can control things. Even after all these years, you think you can shape the outcome. Just let go, enjoy the ride. The only thing that changes is the date on a calendar. The rest is mere window dressing."

Both men were silent for a few minutes, standing side by side and staring into the darkness. The sound of the winter wind filled the air, whipping snow against their faces.

"Have you seen him?" asked Golubev.

"Who is that?" Sokolov said without turning.

"Olek."

Sokolov closed his eyes, exasperated. "Why do you do these things, Sasha? Truly, what is to be gained?"

"I was just wondering if you had seen him. You owe him as much as I do."

Sokolov continued to smoke, uninterested in replying.

Golubev set off into the darkness. "Goodnight, Sok. Enjoy the sunrise."

CHAPTER 14

A BLOOD-CHILLING scream fills the air.

Scrambling, a woman thrusts forward. Her face is covered in blood and dust.

A bag of groceries is smashed on the pavement. Milk bleeds from it.

The police hold her. Thrashing. Wailing. She struggles to break free. "Let me go! Let me go!"

The morning had been peaceful. Peaceful for wartime, that is.

A walk with the dog. A little bit of homework before some screentime. A quiet moment to herself, away from the duties of home life. Little things like this still matter. Proof that life still exists beyond this horror.

Walking home in the sun.

An explosion. The ground shakes.

It was close. But how close? And where?

Walking quickly. Then running.

And then she saw. The assembled crowd. Family and friends rushing to her.

And then the smoke. Fire. Rubble.

The police try to control the chaos as the fire brigade rushes in.

She thrashes, straining to reach them. Tears stream down her face.

This is the day she has witnessed her own death.

Death from above.

Gone.

Son.

Husband.

Mother.

All of them.

Gone.

CHAPTER 15

THE TEAR GAS would only be required once. Colonel Sokolov had made sure of it.

Before going to bed, he had ordered Captain Grigorovich to clear the square the following morning. Given Mikhailovich's increasingly agitated state of mind, it was time to end this "sunrise" charade. Plus, if Golubev was right, these people were laughing at them. And, no matter how he felt about the broader conflict, this sort of disrespect couldn't stand.

Beyond that, Sokolov's orders to Grigorovich were clear: maximum fear with zero casualties. While he wanted to break their will, Sokolov didn't want any propaganda wins for the Nativists. Unnecessary deaths would be powerful communication tools in the hands of the Fascist enemy. "These people need to understand who is in charge," he had said.

Long before dawn, Captain Grigorovich ordered his men into place. Crouched in the shadows, they waited and watched as the townspeople peacefully assembled before first light. This was an exciting mission, and Grigorovich was glad to accept it.

Since the beginning of the War, Grigorovich had viewed the entire Special Operation as an opportunity to prove himself and advance his career. Military battle was how reputations and careers were made. This mission from Sokolov was a perfect opportunity to showcase his wares. And he intended to seize it.

Despite the morning cold, spirits were high amongst the citizens. Afterall, secrets bond people in a way that few other things can.

Mothers pushed prams. Grandparents held hands with children. People smiled and nodded to their neighbours. Old friends in puffer jackets and scarves chit-chatted about nothing in particular. Apart from the War, it was almost idyllic.

Grigorovich's plan was simple: encircle the square and bombard it with gas. But the young captain wasn't a man of half measures. He was a "measure twice, blow it up once" kind of character. This he had learned from his father, who never, ever left anything to chance on their family farm. "Better to bring a tank to a knife fight," he would always say.

On Grigorovich's orders, the amount of gas his men carried that morning was more than one would safely use in an area that size. Far more. But that was the point.

As the first light hit, so too did the gas. Grigorovich smiled. It was beautiful to watch.

Panic took hold as the cannisters landed. In an instant the city square was engulfed in putrid, thick smoke.

In the chaos, parents fumbled for their screaming children. Names of loved ones bounced around the square in terror. The young tried to help the elderly. But quickly, they were also overwhelmed by the enveloping fog.

People scrambled and stumbled in every direction. Coughing. Screaming. Choking. "Air, we need air!"

But the people would not be allowed to disperse. No, they were to suffer. Just as Grigorovich had ordered, all exits from the square had been blocked. Soldiers with riot gear formed a perimeter to keep those trying to flee inside the square. Like a regiment of an ancient Roman legion, the men stood side by side, forming a wall with their shields.

Nobody could get through. The crowd pressed forward in panic, causing those in front to fall and be trampled on the cold, wet and hard ground.

Observing the scene with a grin, Grigorovich ordered the soldiers to fire into the air. It was time to put on a show.

The staccato of machine gun fire came from every direction, echoing around the square. The crowd was surrounded. Panic increased. The noose tightened; the crowd surged.

Maximum fear. Suffocating screams. Chaos.

The stinging, choking gas consumed the entire square.

Anyone stuck inside the cloud was blinded. In some cases, permanently. The frail and enfeebled fell. Some, forever.

Eventually, the firing stopped. Slowly, the gas cleared.

In the clearing air, the horrors presented themselves. Terror and heartbreak in even measure. Coughing, huddled masses littered the square. Mothers on top of their children, desperately trying to shield them.

A younger man was lying face down, blood pouring from the exit wound of an errant bullet.

An old man stood slowly to his feet. Still holding his wife's hand, he tried to pull her up. Then he shook her. Then he wept.

"Get out of here!" Grigorovich yelled, pushing the old man from behind.

The old man stumbled forward, saved from another fall only by the strength of his walking stick. Grigorovich lifted the butt of his gun, preparing to strike the old man again when he was suddenly pushed from behind.

"Leave him alone, you bastard!" came a young, piercing voice. Grigorovich spun on his heels to see a Nativist girl, somewhere in her teen years, her fists clenched. Even though he wasn't a short man, the girl with dark brown hair and flashing blue eyes towered above him.

"Katya!" the old man managed with a cough.

Grigorovich eyed up the girl. "A young feisty one, eh? Just my type," he snickered to one of his nearby soldiers.

Before Grigorovich could continue, Katya rushed to the old man, shielding him from further attacks with her body. "It's okay, it's okay," Katya whispered in the man's ear while stroking his face. Looking back at Grigorovich with contempt, Katya placed the old man's arm over her shoulder and began to slowly walk him from the square.

"Don't you run too far, my little *divchonka*. I'll be seeing you soon," Grigorovich cat-called after her.

Very soon, he thought to himself.

* * *

Slowly but surely, the remaining people went home to safety. Staggering and coughing as they went. Helping one another however they could.

The soldiers shoved those remaining in the square out of the centre, down the narrow alleys and streets. The same alleys and streets they had blocked only minutes before.

Grigorovich stood in the middle of the now-empty square. Surveying the aftermath of his work, he couldn't help but feel pleased with himself. "Job well done, lads! Job well done!" he said to the soldiers as they began the task of cleaning away the dead and injured. He was pleased, but he also knew the protocol and immediately ordered his men into action. Graves were dug. Evidence was swept away. Zero casualties.

But despite Grigorovich's best efforts, the memories would remain. Those would not be swept away so easily.

* * *

In the days after what became known as the "Final Sunrise," military searches and surveillance efforts across the city were increased by Sokolov and his men. While he was frustrated by Grigorovich's lack of restraint, Sokolov ensured the impact of the event did not go to waste.

Random door knocks. Bag searches. Phone checks. Interrogations. Sokolov was utterly determined to break the Fascist cell, and redoubled his efforts to degrade and detect the enemy. Whatever it took.

Those who posted Nativist news or information on Telegram channels were followed and harassed. Anyone found filming or taking photos, especially with non-Motherland-issued equipment, had their phone smashed by military police.

Then the disappearances began.

Slowly at first, but then with gradual momentum. Sometimes they came at night. Windows and doors were kicked in. Men, teens, women and children were dragged from their beds. Screaming, they disappearing into the black night. And vans.

Most returned home. Bruised, but not broken. Some were held indefinitely. Agitators.

A message had been sent. It had also been received, but perhaps not as Sokolov had intended. In the people, hope had not been extinguished. Hidden away in corners of the soul, it flickered. They would remember.

* * *

In the city, faces and hearts hardened once again.

The Invaders could feel it, even if they couldn't see or touch it. Grigorovich tried to dismiss it with bravado when his men spoke of their fears in the mess hall, but even he didn't relish evening patrols or walking home alone.

Shades were pulled tight as soldiers patrolled the empty, snow-filled streets. Though they were alone, they knew they were being watched. Eyes peered and peaked from everywhere. Despite the guns in their hands, the Invaders could feel themselves being hunted. They might have been in control, but they were the ones on display.

The soldiers received no warmth on entry into stores or restaurants. But nor was there any hostility. The service they received was polite, but perfunctory.

"Yes, sir. No, sir. Over there, sir," shopkeepers would say while taking the soldiers' money – their awful, foreign money.

Coffees came to the soldiers cold. "Wartime electricity problems, you see. My apologies, sir. Yes, we will do better."

Plates were dropped accidentally. "Sorry, that was the last meal, I'm afraid, sir."

Patiently and politely, the people waited. It put the Occupying men on edge.

The time would come.

Soon.

And everyone knew it.

* * *

A week later, a video began to circulate via Telegram message.

First, it was sent amongst locals in the city and surrounding areas. Then, it found its way to the soldiers. Then, as these things do, it found its way to the world.

Headlined "Who are the Fascists?" the video played back, in graphic detail, the horrific events from the Final Sunrise. A peaceful crowd was surrounded. Trapped like animals. Tortured. The video showed a soldier smashing the face of a blinded woman as she desperately scrambled to break through the blockade with her daughter.

In his office, Sokolov watched the video dispassionately on his phone. It was just as he'd predicted. Based on what he had seen of events at the time, it was clear to Sokolov that Grigorovich had gone well beyond what he had been ordered. Only now the world knew it too.

"A boy doing a man's job," Sokolov muttered to himself.

Though the official death tally would remain at zero, Sokolov knew the protocols of "clean up" better than anyone. And even he could see the bodies in the footage. More importantly, irrespective of the official story put forward by Central Command, this overreach was a gift to the Nativist propaganda efforts.

Despite his misgivings, Sokolov reassured himself that Mikhailovich would be happy the event was documented for the world to see. Or, more importantly, that it was seen back East, where it undoubtedly would be celebrated.

After the events of Patriots' Day, Mikhailovich only had an audience of one in mind. No doubt, he would view this as another successful inch up the greasy pole of promotion. Furthermore, the combination of the event, video footage and ongoing surveillance sweeps would help Sokolov convince Mikhailovich that all was well in the city. And that was worth something.

It was still early in the morning, with the sun only beginning to peek over the horizon. Sokolov enjoyed the ritual and the discipline of being in the office at first light, even though there was no longer any intelligence benefit. Being alone gave him a chance to reflect. Looking outside, he smiled to himself. White with snow and peaceful, there were no more secret games being played in the square below. Gradually, the town came into view as the sun crept slowly upwards.

Sokolov stopped midway through a sip of his morning

brew, his mouth slightly ajar. A droplet of coffee ran down his chin and dripped onto his white collar.

Against the wall below, where the crowds had gathered only days before, was a message painted in large blue and yellow lettering.

BUT WHO WILL LIBERATE YOU?

Suddenly, Sokolov recognised the vantage point from the Final Sunrise video he had watched earlier. The footage had been taken from inside his office.

CHAPTER 16

Weapons from the West finally start to arrive.

Serious weapons. Long-range weapons.

Thanks to the deliveries, the Reaper's reach is no longer one way. His evil game will now see service returned.

In the Eastern Frontiers, the Invaders press forward but are frustrated. Ground is slowly gained, but at an enormous cost.

The heroes will not go quietly. *Bleed them out. Make them pay.*

Bodies pile in the streets. Dead cities of rubble are protected like prizes.

Who will break first?

A "victory" is claimed over whatever is left in this small pocket of the country. A "Republic" flies its false flag. The news flows East.

Finally, something to show for the effort. Success!

A revised objective – any objective – is better to achieve than none. Even a pyrrhic victory brings fewer consequences for those involved.

Exhausted troops in hollowed-out units limp back East for retooling. Those who are left are outnumbered by those who are gone.

Reinforcements are needed. But who will join a war going so brilliantly?

In the Occupied South, explosions hit nerve and command centres. For the first time since the madness began, they're coming from the West.

Satellites triangulate positions.

Ammunition dumps explode in distant bases. Shells and advanced missiles strike in the night. Troops are rattled. Leaders wonder what can be done.

Maximum fear.

A fightback? Is it possible?

Liberation. In their mind's eye, it can be seen.

And that is all that matters.

CHAPTER 17

The winter blizzard had lasted for a week and showed no signs of abating.

Buildings in the town were snowed in, but persistent shovelling and ploughing from the Invaders kept the city functioning as best as possible in the conditions. Locals shovelled too, but for themselves and their neighbours. Anything that would assist the objectives of the Occupiers was studiously avoided. Soldiers would return to recently dug-out places to find their work filled in. With little choice, Grigorovich would order his frustrated men to dig it out once again. It was thankless and backbreaking work in trying conditions. Inevitably, Invader morale began to dip.

Most critically, the work at the nuclear plant had to continue without impediment.

For all of Mikhailovich's tough talk, he had no appetite for accidents, particularly while winter made leaving the city difficult. Access points and flow of traffic were prioritised by Mikhailovich's men to ensure those who needed to attend the plant could. And despite the temptation and hushed debate amongst the Union members, no sabotage was attempted.

The snow had also made Eastern rail links less reliable. This meant shortages of creature comforts such as whisky and vodka. Meals became more basic too. All of it added up to an increasingly grumpy unit of soldiers. Promised fortune and glory, none of them had signed up for *this*. It was all supposed to be over in the autumn, with winter spent back at home as celebrated heroes. And yet here they were, hunched over weak borsch in the snow and miles away from warm bodies that could comfort them.

The regular power outages didn't help matters either. The fact that outages somehow kept happening to the infantry barracks – but never the headquarters – led to even more grumbling and some dark conspiracy theories.

"We live like dogs out here, while they sit in comfort and warmth," said one young soldier to another.

"I bet they are having roast beef in there," another said while stirring his spoon in the thin broth in front of him.

Grigorovich would reassure his men that it was all just a coincidence or the product of shoddy Nativist buildings or Fascist wiring. Though even he had to wonder at times.

Throughout the day, Grigorovich and his men patrolled the empty, windswept streets. With most locals staying home due to the conditions, and sensing the brooding of his men, Grigorovich authorised smaller and less regular patrols. It seemed wasteful to have men walking in sub-zero conditions for little to no purpose. Grigorovich knew a cold man was worse for morale than a hungry one. Besides, as far as he could tell, the town had been subdued since the Final Sunrise.

Though he was cold and found the quarrelling men under his control to be tiresome, Grigorovich couldn't help but admire his own work that day. He was certain this would make the senior brass back home notice him. Who knew how far it had gone up? Maybe all the way? Grigorovich had heard The Commander took personal interest in activities of note. It was a thrilling thought.

Mikhailovich had honoured Grigorovich for his efforts in front of a general meeting of the entire military deployment. It was the proudest day of Grigorovich's life.

Grigorovich had heard that some officers, including Sokolov, had said he'd gone too far in his methods. But they were weak and meek. Weakness only leads to more weakness. This was what The Commander said. And this was precisely what he told his men.

"Sir, it's absolutely freezing!" Private Talinevsky said through his balaclava.

Grigorovich was instantly transported back to the cold

street he was patrolling and away from his self-gratifying naval gazing. Because of the noise generated by the gale, he signalled with his hands for Talinevsky to repeat himself.

"I said, it is absolutely *freezing*!" repeated Talinevsky, leaning in closely to his captain.

Grigorovich squinted as he surveyed the landscape. The storm was whipping snow against his exposed nose and eyes. Talinevsky was right; it *was* freezing. Though it had been cold all day, this was something else entirely. The blizzard had come seemingly from nowhere.

Now that Grigorovich thought about it, it was impossible to tell where they were in the city. A total whiteout was underway. He looked around for a tell-tale landmark or something to orient himself with, but to no avail.

"We must get inside," Talinevsky pressed.

"I can't feel my face. My hands are already gone . . ." said Private Badagovich, standing nearby.

Grigorovich nodded. Their predicament would become terminal with the wrong decision making. Grigorovich understood from previous deployments that these conditions were enough to kill a man who was exposed long enough. But he didn't want to induce panic with the younger, inexperienced men in his command. He maintained a steady demeanour.

"This way!" he signalled to the men with confidence.

In truth, Grigorovich had no idea where they were headed. But he knew the city streets were narrow enough that, eventually, they would hit a structure of some sort. Grigorovich just hoped it was one with a welcoming door.

As they walked, the forbidding snowstorm intensified further.

"Keep going," Grigorovich muttered to himself, checking periodically to make sure he hadn't lost the two privates. Any deaths would be awful for his official record.

Suddenly, up ahead Grigorovich could see something. Each step closer revealed it a little more. A building. Administration HQ? No, wait, a house! The chimney puffed faint smoke into the white inferno. Someone was home. A saviour!

Reaching the building, Grigorovich bashed on the door. No answer.

Inspecting the barred doors and windows, his heart sank a little. Breaking in would not be easy. He bashed on the door again with his fist, this time more in hope than expectation. Feeling the quiet desperation of the two young men behind him, Grigorovich couldn't face them.

Suddenly, a lock snapped. The door creaked slightly open.

"Hello!" Grigorovich yelled over the sound of the wind. "Hello, we are sorry to bother you! We are lost in the blizzard. Would you be so kind as to let us in, so we can connect with our military unit?"

"Oh, get in here, you silly boys!" replied a woman's voice warmly.

Not needing a second invitation, the three men poured

inside, and the door slammed shut behind them.

The three soldiers stood in the entrance hall of a small home. Through the circular window of the door, they could see a raging fireplace.

Grigorovich turned to see an old woman latching the door firmly shut. The locks snapped once again. Bent over and slouched, the tiny woman was dressed in a heavy coat, a grey shawl over her white hair and large protruding nose.

"Madam, we thank you for your generosity," Grigorovich said.

The two privates knocked the snow from their shoulders, faces and boots. Their gratitude was evident in their energy.

"And what are three handsome soldiers doing out in these conditions?" the old woman asked.

"These are our orders, I'm afraid, ma'am. Rain, hail, or storm, we are obligated to fulfil our duty. I am Captain Grigorovich, and these are Privates Talinevsky and Badagovich," he said with unfailing politeness.

The two fresh-faced privates, both with matching buzzcuts, nodded and offered polite hellos. If it wasn't for Talinevsky's blue eyes and Badagovich's brown, they'd have been impossible to tell apart.

"Captain! Why, you are an important man. And so young," said the woman.

Grigorovich couldn't help but blush a little, though he wasn't sure why.

"Come, come! Get out of these coats and get inside," she said.

Walking inside to the warmth of the fire was a godsend. The privates, having lost all inhibition, rushed towards the lapping flames to unthaw their hands.

Grigorovich surveyed the quaint house. It was basic, Empire-era construction, but well-appointed and maintained. In the circumstances, it was an absolute palace.

"And we didn't get your name, I am afraid, madam? This is most rude of me," said Grigorovich.

"Call me Baba," she laughed.

"Baba?" Grigorovich smiled. He didn't know why – maybe it was being so far away from home – but even hearing that word out loud felt reassuring.

"And you live alone, Baba?" he tried to inquire innocently.

"Oh, you have nothing to fear here, Captain," said Baba with a wink, her lined face scrunching pleasantly. With a gold-and-metal-toothed grin, Baba threw her head to the corner of the room. Following her eyeline, Grigorovich turned to see a small flag of the Old Empire hanging on the wall. He smiled. "A patriot!" he said.

Baba grinned her appreciation at this honourable acknowledgment. "Now, would you like some borsch? Baba's special! Just like home," she said, walking into the nearby kitchen. "And don't tell me you aren't hungry! I have too much already. And you boys are frozen to your bone marrow."

"Borsch . . ." said Private Badagovich longingly. The young soldier looked at Grigorovich with begging eyes. It had been so long since they had eaten properly.

"Well, Baba, if you insist. But we wouldn't want to impose," replied Grigorovich.

"Ha! Keep calling me 'Baba' and I will let you move in," she said while sticking her head back out in the living area. With a playful chuckle, she darted back into the kitchen to continue her important work. "I haven't heard that word in years! They all moved away, all too busy to call," she yelled from inside the kitchen as she stirred the hearty soup.

Minutes later, the old woman came out with a large, steaming pot.

"Sit, sit! Come on, this is not a military barracks. Hats off at my table," she commanded the three men.

Hot, delicious steam filled the room quickly. The richness of the beetroot broth hung in the air. And what was that? Beef? Actual beef?

This is heaven, Badagovich thought to himself. The smell was so overwhelmingly good that he nearly tripped over Talinevsky as the pair rushed to the table.

"You are good boys," Baba said, ladling the soup into the large ceramic bowls laid out in front of them. "Loyal servants. Protecting the Motherland. Restoring the Empire. You deserve some old-fashioned, Empire-strength borsch."

The three men ate greedily. Maybe it was the cold, but

the quality of the borsch was unbelievable. Moans of sheer joy filled the small, warm room. For three young men a long way from home, this was nothing short of heaven.

"Baba makes a good borsch, no?" the old woman said with a toothy, wrinkled grin.

"Oh, I thought my Baba knew how to make it. But, oh. Oh, this borsch!" said Talinevsky, slurping at his spoon.

Grigorovich laughed and smiled. These were days when life almost seemed normal. And he had to admit, it was damn good borsch.

Baba was thrilled to see the young men enjoying her cooking, and the company from three strapping lads was most welcome. It had been a lonely winter, and the War meant she couldn't see her family in the East or West. So here she had sat, all alone.

Before they could ask, she topped up the bowls of the three men. Grigorovich briefly feigned protest, while Talinevsky and Bagadovich didn't even bother with the pleasantries.

She watched the men eating with a grin. "Oh, it is so good to see such strong young men. And to be at my table! Oh, it has been years. How lucky I am! God has smiled down on me."

The men filled their bowls again and again until there was nothing left in Baba's big pot. Pushing his bowl to the side, a satisfied and replenished Grigorovich looked outside. The snow was lighter now, and the city was visible. Due to the disorientation of the storm, Grigorovich now realised they had accidently walked to an outer ring of the city. Though he couldn't understand how it had happened, it was good to know where they were.

He looked at his watch. It was time to switch patrols, and the three men had a long walk back to base they would need to make in quick time.

"Baba, I wish we could stay, but we must leave. Duty calls," Grigorovich said, pointing to his watch.

Heartened and warmed, the three men walked out onto the street. Stepping back into the cold, fresh air, Grigorovich felt reborn. With the storm now passed, the snow had stopped falling, meaning it would be a pleasant walk back to the barracks.

"May the Motherland protect you," Baba said, her lined face creasing into a golden, gap-toothed smile.

"And you," said Grigorovich, placing his woollen hat over his head and ears.

Grigorovich turned and jogged to catch up to the two privates already making footmarks in the snow. Ahead of him, Grigorovich could hear Talinevsky whistling the tune of the Motherland.

Grigorovich smiled and sucked in the cool winter air. Things were looking up.

* * *

Four soldiers, each on motorised snow scooters, came driving past. They had been searching for hours, but finally the missing patrol had been located.

After noticing a helmet on the ground to his left, the soldier riding on the trailing scooter hit the brakes.

Honking his horn, the soldier waved to the three scooters ahead. He'd found them! The men hit their brakes and began to circle back.

Parking his scooter against the curb, the young private stepped down onto the snow-covered street before the others could return to his position.

In front of him lay the frozen, rigid bodies of Grigorovich, Talinevsky and Bagadovich.

CHAPTER 18

They're after us.

Officially, the deaths of Captain Grigorovich and Privates Badagovich and Talinevsky had been listed under "misadventure."

But the men knew better. This was no accident. Rumours swirled about Grigorovich being found face down in vomit. Had he been poisoned? And if so, by whom?

They're after us.

Was it local Fascists or a band of marauding resistance fighters on the city outskirts? The soldiers debated which would be more concerning. Either way, the implications were serious. Nobody wanted to die in this hellish winter so far from home.

I want to go home.

Beyond Grigorovich's possible murder by local partisans,

word began to filter through the unit that the broader War was turning against them.

We are going to die here.

Those who hadn't yet lost their nerve dismissed this information as Nativist propaganda designed to spook them. But others were not so sure. There had been lots of talk of military failures across the south and west of the country. And of course, there was the shambolic and failed attempts to take the Capital.

They're bleeding us out slowly. And there are more of them.

In quiet corners, over cheap vodka, the Motherland soldiers would whisper of a rumoured counter-offensive being planned by the enemy.

"Have you heard the Nativists are planning to move South?"

"Yes. But when?"

Rumours were traded as intrigue before being repeated back and confirmed as fact.

"They want the nuclear plant back; their Western partners are demanding it. This city is located on a strategic river, you know."

"And what of this new Western weaponry? I hear it is devastatingly effective."

"Have you heard another general has died? This time in the East? How many is that now? Fifteen? Twenty? How many do we have left?"

"Maybe if they lose enough generals, they'll let us live too? Surely, we've lost enough."

"Do you think we can go home soon?"

From that point onward, more soldiers went on patrol and then disappeared into the night, never to return.

Some men drifted away, hoping to be presumed lost. Others likely met nastier ends.

It was now impossible to tell which was which.

They were after them.

CHAPTER 19

The freshly printed passport sat on Oksana's desk.

Everyone in the city had one now and, thanks to the latest Ordinance, it was compulsory to always carry them. Oksana understood that the latest, utterly capricious law was less about identification and more about humiliation and subservience.

Her passport had arrived via delivery a few days before, but she hadn't looked at it until now. She knew that by refusing to carry this ridiculous, offensive document she was breaching the new identification Ordinance, only she didn't care.

Opening the package to see the emblazoned logo of the Motherland staring back at her – on a document bearing her name – would make it feel too real. And what more could they do to her that they hadn't already done?

The new Motherland passports had been issued ahead

of the upcoming Liberation Ballot. Signs had gone up around the city in anticipation of the supposed referendum. The vote, if one could call it that, would decide whether the city and the broader region should formally "re-join" the Motherland. This was to be the final, unbreakable step in Motherfication.

To Oksana, it was the most offensive part of it all. The Motherland's armies were murdering her people, imprisoning her town, erasing her culture – and now they expected her to count herself as one of them? It was incredulous.

While everyone knew the process would be nothing more than a sham vote, the complete departure from reality in the election messaging was extraordinary. Even by the Motherland's standards of propaganda, this was a step above.

Posters in the red, blue and white – colours of the Motherland – adorned every street post and corner.

"Secure your Liberation! Vote Yes!"

"Every vote counts! Do not leave matters to chance!"

"One big family. One big Motherland!"

"Save lives, join the Motherland!"

"Peace through unity! Vote Yes!"

Oksana couldn't help but partly admire the sheer audacity of it. *Only a cynic could believe a lie that passionately*, she thought to herself.

She studied the small passport booklet, running her fingers over the raised golden lettering of the Motherland's national insignia. Whatever this symbol had once meant to anyone, to people like Oleksandr, it only represented one thing now: hate.

Oksana wondered how the War and Occupation would end – *if* they would ever end. Could this type of madness ever be reasoned with or brought to heel? And if this obnoxious referendum law was passed, as seemed inevitable, what would happen next?

Sham or not, according to law they'd all be formally part of the Motherland's orbit, not that they weren't already. But like an unwanted marriage, the referendum had a sense of trapped finality about it, beyond what Oksana was experiencing now. It was chilling.

She knew that a successful referendum would give the Invaders scope to lay claim to her area – and anyone in it – as part of any negotiated peace deal between the two nations. The idea of a so-called "status quo settlement" – one that had her trapped on *this* side of line – made her feel sick with grief and worry.

Oksana could see the local resistance movement was gathering momentum. But even so, she wasn't confident it was strong enough to throw off the shackles and expel the Occupiers. To have any chance of success, they needed more time. And even still, she understood these were civilians operating in a loose network of nuisance. These people were not soldiers. As brave as they were, they needed the equipment to get the job done.

No, there would need to be serious fighting, military fighting, to break The Commander's evil grip on the city. Even then it would be difficult. And that wasn't even considering the prospect of a potential nuclear catastrophe, should anything go wrong.

Oksana knew it was important to remain positive even in the face of uncertainty or unspeakable odds. That was what she always told her Union members. But from time to time, on days like this, she struggled to believe her own words. And she was tired. Like everyone around her, Oksana was so damn tired.

But what else was there to do? To think otherwise would be to give in. And that just wasn't an option. She would die first.

Her thoughts drifted to the Homeland's armies, still fighting bravely across the country. She wondered about her brother, Dmytro. She'd had received no word on his safety since the Occupation started and he deployed to fight. But Dmytro was a stubborn bastard. The Invaders would need a second army to get rid of him, Oksana assured herself.

She'd heard the rumours of a counter-offensive being planned by the Homeland armies. According to the information, the President had ordered for the South – with its critical seaports and economic assets – to be retaken as an urgent priority. That would mean Heryvin.

When she was feeling positive, Oksana pictured the Homeland army, and Dmytro, coming to stage a genuine liberation of the city. Picturing her brother's face was one of the few thoughts that kept her going through the fatigue and the terror.

It would happen. It *had* to happen. But when? How long could they hang on?

A shadow darkened her office door. "I see your documentation has arrived, Miss Shevchenko," said Mikhailovich, startling her out of her reverie.

Before she could invite him in, the Lieutenant General was already taking a seat in front of her. "I hope this is a good time," he said.

"Talk of the wolf," Oksana said, tossing her passport just enough to slide it away from her. It stopped on the edge of the desk in front of Mikhailovich.

"I trust all is well?" he said, looking down at the document in front of him.

"Wonderful."

"And the nuclear plant and dam are operating to their appropriate levels?"

"We've had to reduce output slightly to accommodate for the longer than usual freezing of the river," Oksana replied. "But this is normal and accounted for, under our standard practices and procedures. But, of course, you know all this."

"And what of your members? I see absenteeism has steadily fallen. What about things that cannot be measured – morale, for example?"

"Morale?"

"Well, how are your people feeling?"

"You mean other than fearful of being gassed if they walk outside? Beyond that, I imagine they're feeling wonderful."

Mikhailovich smirked. It was clear to Oksana he had something on his mind. He wasn't one to pop into her office for chit-chat.

"Comrade Lieutenant General, is there something that brings you here today? Surely there is nothing that could not wait until our official briefing."

"Very well, Miss Shevchenko. I must tell you that I have come across some most disturbing news. I hear talk of a major sabotage at this facility of ours."

"Oh, yes? How disturbed you must be."

"Yes. The sabotage, I'm afraid, relates to the ongoing activities of this plant – and, more importantly, the water supply and the good functioning of the river itself." His eyes narrowed with contempt. "As you know, there has been increased criminal and Fascist activity in the city. There have been murders, as you know."

"Indeed, I do."

"On account of this heightened activity, I have no choice but to give greater credence to this new intelligence. Given it comes from, shall we say, closely placed sources."

Oksana sat back and crossed her arms. "And? You are here to interrogate me and see if I have any information as to this supposed 'plot' of yours?"

"Well, Miss Shevchenko, it is not information I seek.

Information I have. No, the purpose of this meeting is to deliver a warning."

"A warning? To whom?"

"Should something happen to this facility, or to the ongoing water supply flowing south to the Peninsula, well, I would be forced to assume that this was an inside job and act accordingly."

Oksana paused. "An inside job?"

"Yes, an inside job executed by a Fascist cell operating within this city. Within this very facility. Fascists that have infiltrated their way to the very top, I could only assume."

"And what is it you think is about to happen here?"

"There are plots, Miss Shevchenko. Dark plots. Plots intended to injure, or worse, kill those who wish to join the Motherland. There are moves to harm those who yearn for freedom from the Fascists and for Liberation." His face darkened. "I will not – I *cannot* sit idly by and allow such an unspeakable thing to happen."

"And what proof do you have of this? Other than your paranoid fantasies?" Oksana asked.

He stared at her intently. "I assure you, I am neither paranoid, nor a fantasist. The Fascist activity in the city speaks for itself. Likewise, the intelligence. Madam Secretary, this Union of yours is a hotbed of agitation and agitators. I have tolerated it, but even my tolerance has its limits."

"These would be exhausted agitators," Oksana replied.

"I'm not sure where they'd find the time or the energy for these plots of yours. There have been several close calls in safety at the plant as it is. Frankly, our members are near death trying to prevent disaster – and it's a miracle we haven't had one already. But please – tell me what you think our Union members are likely to do."

"Miss Shevchenko, I am not about to divulge what I know, how I know it, or freely give ideas you have not yet conceived on your own. I am tasked with maintaining the safety and functioning of this facility and the criticality of the ongoing water supply to the Peninsula. Everything else is subordinate to this aim. The water must flow. The power must stay on. These are my orders. And they will be fulfilled."

"And we have fulfilled our end of that bargain. Such as it is," Oksana replied, her tone icy.

"Know this: any disruption to or disturbance of the water – any at all – will be met with a full and forceful response. I think by now you realise I am not a man to be tested."

Oksana sat in her chair. Silent. Unmoving. She decided carefully how she would respond. "Your warning is noted, Lieutenant General. But I assure you, you are looking in the wrong place. Our members simply want a quiet life. They do not yearn for battle. Or trouble. It may seem trite to you, but we love our land. We would not seek to destroy it, even if it had the correlated benefit of making us free. This might be your conquest, but this is our home."

"Ha! Well, if it's truly a quiet life your members want, then they will have it," Mikhailovich said.

"Once again, we usually find a way to agree. Though perhaps not for the reasons we both believe," Oksana said with a sigh.

"Then our business is concluded," said Mikhailovich, standing to leave. When he reached the door, he turned back to Oksana.

"Oh, and Miss Shevchenko, do be sure to vote in the upcoming Liberation elections. It is a secret ballot, of course, but secrets can sometimes find their way out."

"I look forward to exercising my vote, Comrade." She paused and cocked an eyebrow. "I trust you have someone taking you home? It can be easy to get lost in the snow at this time of year."

The officer stiffened. Looking down at his pistol, he smiled before looking up. "I look forward to you joining the Motherland, Miss Shevchenko. There, you will have all the very same rights and protections as our citizens."

And with that, Mikhailovich walked from the room.

* * *

Walking home along the bank of the frozen river, Oksana turned the conversation with Mikhailovich over in her mind. The air was crisp, but with no snow falling, it was unusually easy walking on the freshly swept sidewalk.

Despite the improved weather conditions, which often coaxed people out of their homes to walk pets or run errands, the street was empty in both directions.

What does he know? Oksana asked herself. *Perhaps nothing.*

Even though Mikhailovich was no mastermind, Oksana understood a man of his ambition and volatility was capable of anything. It was possible he was on a fishing expedition looking for information, or had hoped to prompt paranoid introspection – the kind of introspection she was engaging in now.

Fuelling these types of rumours was also an effective way to get Union members to turn on one another. Or, heaven forbid, encourage them to become Collaborators.

Still, Oksana wondered what he knew. The idea that one of her own was working with him was impossible to rule out. As much as it pained her, Oksana had to concede that maybe there was a rat amongst them.

"A little late to be recruiting members!" a voice called out in the twilight, breaking Oksana's concentration.

She turned to see a figure walking towards her in the dying light and smiled as she recognised Elena, dressed in a black hooded puffer jacket. It was nice to see a friendly face. They felt few and far between these days.

"Principal Kovalenko, how are you?" Oksana said, embracing the older woman in a warm hug.

"I am well, my dear. And how is my favourite former

student?" Elena said, still embracing Oksana but pulling her head back slightly so she could study her face.

Oksana laughed. "I can't still be your favourite. Not after all these years."

"What is it they say about old habits?"

Oksana loosened the hug but kept holding Elena by the hands. "They die hard," she said.

"Like all of us," Elena replied, raising her brows.

Oksana smiled softly. She had always loved Elena Kovalenko. She was Oksana's favourite teacher and a woman she deeply admired. Elena had also been close with her father when they were young, and that made the woman feel even more familiar. It was a feeling Oksana enjoyed, particularly now.

Elena looked at Oksana. Even in the dark, she could see her former student was tired. Her youthful zest looked frayed at the edges, and who could blame her? They were all utterly exhausted.

"And how are you, my dear Oksana?" Elena followed up.

"Well, you know . . ."

"Yes. Yes, of course, I do." She paused for a moment. "And how goes the work of the plant?"

"It goes on. With reluctance or otherwise, it goes on."

Elena nodded slowly. She understood the difficult situation Oksana and her comrades were in. "Your father would be proud of you, Oksana Shevchenko."

The Union leader sighed. "Sometimes I wonder."

Elena came closer to the young woman. "Oksana, my dear, please do not think for a moment that your good work goes unnoticed or is not appreciated."

"Sometimes I wonder if I am making the right choice," Oksana said. "I almost feel like a Collaborator. I work for them, and they achieve their goals. But if I don't, then what is left?"

"You are your father's daughter. He died protecting us all. Just as you are protecting us now."

"I don't know . . ."

Elena looked intently into Oksana's eyes. "Do not fall for the pathetic smears of the Empire. You know in your heart what is true. You father is a hero.

"On the night of The Accident, he made sure every single Union member who could be saved made it out of the facility. He could have survived; he could have chosen himself – but he didn't. And in doing so, he gave his own life. The town was saved. *You* were saved, my dear Oksana." She looked into her former pupil's eyes. "Oh, how he adored you. You were the apple of his eye. And how he would admire your strength today." She squeezed Oksana's hands firmly.

Oksana smiled and looked at her feet, a little embarrassed. "There are days when I wish he was here. Sometimes I try to remember his face from my memories. But I don't know if they are my own or what I have seen in pictures or heard in stories. And yet I still miss him. Not the hero in the local legend. Not the brilliant engineer or the brave conscript. I miss the father who held me when I fell and scraped my knee. Or sang me to sleep when I was scared of the monsters under my bed. And the memories we never got to make . . . well, I miss those more than anything."

"There are not two versions of the man, my dear. The father who loved you and the brave man who sacrificed himself are one and the same," Elena said gently.

Oksana nodded, a small smile appearing on her face before disappearing just as quickly as it came. "And then, if I'm honest, sometimes I feel his shadow on me. It's as though I will forever be measured against an impossible standard. Against a myth. My father is somehow in the air of this city, both nowhere and everywhere at the same time. I feel like he would know what to do. He would have a solution for fighting these bastards or forcing them to concede. He would save us. And then, when I am alone . . . I feel angry that he isn't here to tell us what to do." She looked up at the older woman, eyes brimming with tears. "I know that is an awful thing to say out loud."

Elena felt a pang in her heart. "My sweet girl. You do more for us than you realise. You stand guard against those who would take us beyond the brink of madness." She kept eyes fixed tightly on Oksana. "It seems a Shevchenko has always been this town's guardian angel. And now, rightly or wrongly, it falls to you. I know you did not ask for this task. No true patriot ever does. But I know of your strength and courage,

Oksana. And because of this, I know you will prevail. And so will we all."

"Sometimes I wonder if Oleksandr is right. Perhaps we should make peace. Maybe it would be safer for everyone. Maybe we can find a way to co-exist."

Elena's face hardened. "Oleksandr would be better off repaying his own debts. He was there that night too. And he knows what happened all too well. He was the last one inside. The last man Timofei went back for." She paused, looking at Oksana. Do you not know this story?"

"My mother said some things. But she was so sad. And drunk."

No doubt she was, Elena thought to herself, *considering the horrors she had to live through*. "Then I will tell you what I know," she said to Oksana. "The emergency shutdown and override panel was located in the part of the nuclear plant that was already burning. We don't know for certain, of course, but it seems that room had been irradiated by the core leak. Anyone in there was likely dead, and anyone going in there would likely last only minutes. Tell me, in the event of a disaster – who would you expect to pull that switch?"

Oksana thought for a moment. "Well, things are different now – structurally and technologically, of course. But the code amongst workers is simple: whoever is on duty, they stay until the job is done. No matter what. We all know that. It's part of the Sister and Brotherhood."

Elena nodded. "This was Oleksandr's part of the plant, not your father's. It was his job to pull that emergency switch should something go wrong, nobody else's. Timofei was outside, waiting. But he knew something was wrong. So, he went back. And he did what Oleksandr couldn't, or wouldn't, do. And only one of them came out."

Oksana stood silent for a moment, stunned. "I . . . I had no idea."

Elena nodded again and smiled weakly. "So Olek, of all people, should understand the power of sacrifice."

"And loss, perhaps? He seems so . . . sad."

"Grief. Guilt. They can consume you. But Oleksandr's problem is that he believes he can wish bad things away. But that is impossible, I'm afraid. Evil does not just disappear because we want it to. We can't wish it away or reason with it. So we do what we can do. We pull the switch. We do what's right – or try to, anyway."

"So, you think Papa did the right thing?"

"Yes, my dear. That is what bravery is. It's doing the right thing by the many, even if it means paying a personal cost. Or, in your father's case, the ultimate cost." She closed her eyes, letting out a long breath before she continued. "Now, I do not believe it will come to that same choice for you – but to give in now would be to lose everything. We need you, Oksana Shevchenko."

A small smile appeared on the young woman's lips.

"And as for Oleksandr," Elena added, "he'd do well to take a leaf from his granddaughter's book."

Oksana's smile broke out into a grin. "And how is young Katya? I've not seen her in a while. A brilliant young girl! The best young summer work experience cadet we've had in years. She knows more about nuclear physics than I do!"

"I must admit, she's well on her way to favourite status."

"Well, she will find that title passionately defended!" Oksana declared.

The two women laughed together.

"Like you, she has bravery beyond her years. The young people today, they give me hope," Elena said.

Oksana smiled warmly and nodded in the affirmative.

"It is getting late. And you need some sleep, Madam Secretary," Elena said, looking at her fitness watch. "And I need to get some steps!"

Oksana and Elena hugged again.

"It is good to see you, Principal," Oksana said.

"Take care, my dear."

As Elena disappeared into the night, Oksana looked back over the frozen river towards the nuclear plant. She wondered what her father would do.

The Fascists Must Go! read a sign on the nearby post. Finally, there was a cause Oksana could support.

* * *

Mikhailovich sat in his office alone, contemplating.

She's lying. She has to be, he thought.

There was too much evidence for her not to know about this plot. Otherwise, what sort of leader was she? And he wasn't going to be made a fool of. Not again. No, this time he would stop her once and for all.

The large yellow envelope had been left at the usual spot a week earlier. Only this occasion, his Union source didn't attend. Without any context or explanation from his source, Mikhailovich had been forced to dissect the materials on his own. It was frustrating, but a good source was a good source. And this was certainly high-quality stuff.

Inside the envelope had been a printed spreadsheet, an order manifest for the nuclear plant. And a note. A note he had been studying and contemplating for days.

The drums are en route. Hopefully the ducks can still be of assistance. We know they are for us!

The first part made sense, given Mikhailovich's professional background. The source had highlighted two new orders in the dam and plant order book manifest, which Mikhailovich had studied intently. The first was for a massive order of hydrogen cyanide, a precursor to many chemical compounds. Mikhailovich knew this to be produced on an industrial scale, for use particularly in mining and plastics. More importantly, Mikhailovich remembered from his military academy days that hydrogen cyanide had been historically used in chemical warfare. A dangerous and deadly poison in the wrong hands, it was designated as a military-grade agent.

The second order was for an even larger quantity of benzene. This was easily found as a mass-produced precursor chemical for other industrial processes. A highly flammable and light chemical, benzene would float on top of water quite easily.

When put together, it was obvious what these terrorists were planning.

Poison. And fire.

The destruction of the dam, a poisoning of the waterflow. An end to his leadership.

"These people are animals," Mikhailovich said to himself.

Satisfied enough with his detective work, he rocked back in his seat, reflecting on what would be a breakthrough in his attempts to disrupt the Fascists and perhaps the key to successfully completing his mission. Humming "Hymn of the Motherland" to himself, Mikhailovich daydreamed a little about his triumphant return home. "Arise, General Mikhailovich," he said to himself.

He thought about the glory of accomplishing this Special Operation with aplomb when another memory entered his mind, about the last time he was to be rewarded with praise from the East. And instead, he was met with mockery. And shame.

These terrorists have to be stopped, he thought. And, if need be, he would stop them himself. They would *not* make a fool of him again.

Pouring himself a whisky, Mikhailovich took a deep breath to calm himself down. It would be okay. The humiliation of Patriots' Day couldn't be repeated. This time, he had the advantage. Unlike that idiot Sokolov, he'd cracked the Nativist inner circle, as well as their code. Victory, and her head, would be his.

But, Mikhailovich had to admit there was one thing bothering him. As much as he thought he understood the core elements of their plan, not everything in the intelligence made total sense.

Ducks?

CHAPTER 20

The video had been seen millions of times before it had been censored.

And by then, the stories were well spread and reported in the press. Which was the intent. This was viral, shareable brutality.

Depraved. Inhuman. Unthinkable. Unspeakable.

A prisoner can be seen. A non-combatant in the fatigues of the Homeland.

Six men pin him down.

He begs.

A soldier takes out a knife.

Aiming low, he cuts deeply. Fulsomely. Carving away.

Screams.

Thrashing.

Mutilation.

The world is aghast. But when does it stay this way? When will it see what is happening?

In the Homeland, a people bleed.

If only it could be unseen. If only it wasn't true.

But names would be taken.

Atonement was coming.

If not today, then tomorrow.

And if not tomorrow . . .

Soon.

CHAPTER 21

"And when will the results be in, Comrade Colonel?" asked Mikhailovich.

With his back turned to Sokolov, the Lieutenant General was looking out the window of his office into the darkness of the evening. His hands were clasped behind his back.

Sokolov was leaning against the wall in the corner of the room. He was smoking, as usual, while casually scrolling through his phone. "Surely you are not expecting anything other than a landslide in the affirmative, Comrade Lieutenant General?" he said, exhaling.

"Yes, well, it is best to have these matters confirmed before taking them for granted," Mikhailovich said, still staring outside. He was tense. While he knew Sokolov was right – this really was an unlosable election – it didn't make him any less nervous. Those Nativist savages were up to something. He could feel it.

Sokolov shrugged his shoulders. He had been around long enough to understand what a ballot looked like in the Motherland.

"And what to make of the streets today?" Mikhailovich asked.

"What is there to make?" Sokolov replied.

"It was quiet, was it not?"

Sokolov drew from his cigarette slowly. "Per your orders, sir. No trouble." He held the smoke in his lungs.

A few seconds passed before Mikhailovich turned around to look at Sokolov. "Be that as it may, you did not sense something . . . wrong?"

He really is paranoid, Sokolov thought. "There was no trouble, sir. This is all we could hope for on a day such as this. And it was all achieved without incident. You should be proud. This is a tremendous career success, one that I'm sure will not go unnoticed by superiors back East!"

Mikhailovich was not convinced. "Yes. Without incident." He paused. "And how goes your investigation into the planned sabotage of the river system and dam infrastructure? As you can imagine, this is of most concern to me and our direct reporting lines in the East."

"As I reported to you yesterday, there is nothing we've discovered that can support the intelligence you have received."

"Nothing you've found *so far*," Mikhailovich corrected him.

Sokolov nodded. There was no point arguing. "Given the concern, we are continuing to investigate it. Rest assured, Comrade Lieutenant General, if there are large batches of poison in this city, they will be found. Furthermore, any plan to move such a quantity of materials into the city could not be done without major arterial and logistical support. We do not believe the Fascists have this capability.

"Furthermore," Sokolov continued, "any attempts to stop the flow of water, even a major destruction of the canal system, could easily be corrected. At this stage, we consider an attack improbable."

Mikhailovich paused, taking in the report. "And what of a release of irradiated materials from the plant? It would be a simple thing to damage the facility holding the spent fuel rods. Surely you have considered this possibility? That would be 'yellow', would it not?" Mikhailovich finally said.

"I have. But this would require an act of self-harm and self-sabotage on such a scale that appears out of character."

"Out of character? Really, for such savages?"

"Nothing so far would suggest they seek a scorched-earth approach to their resistance. It would seem against their primary interests, which is the regaining of their land. As impossible as this is, that is what they want."

Mikhailovich sniffed in disgust. "You give far too much

credit to the Nativists, Colonel. These people, such as they are, are animals. Dogs. And, do not forget, they are led by an ambitious agitator. An agitator with a bloodline." He carried his eyes to the window, onto the town below. "Colonel, does the term 'duck' mean anything to you?"

"Duck? I'm afraid I'll need more context."

"How could a duck, if that is a code word of sorts, help you?" Mikhailovich followed up.

Sokolov paused and thought for a moment. "There is an old term within prisons, but I'm not sure it is of relevance."

Mikhailovich turned with sudden interest. "Go on."

"In the gulags, prisoners would refer to the guards that helped them as 'ducks'. So, if you successfully convinced a guard to help you, that guard was a duck. And, eventually, the aim was to corrupt the guard to such an extent that you could blackmail him. Once you owned that guard through blackmail, the 'duck' was said to be 'downed'."

"Hmm . . . how interesting."

"Criminals are nothing, if not creative. Is there a reason you ask?"

"No reason that concerns you, Sokolov. Speaking of birds, Comrade Colonel – tell me, where is your pigeon of a friend?"

Sokolov paused. "Who?"

"Major Golubev, where is he?"

"Oh?"

"Well, that's what his name is derived from: the pigeon," said Mikhailovich, amused with himself. He turned to face Sokolov. "And you know what they call pigeons?"

Sokolov was unsure where Mikhailovich was going with this. "Stupid?"

"The rats of the sky!" Mikhailovich said with relish.

Sokolov smirked, joining in the joke only half-heartedly. "Major Golubev is on duty, sir. In the absence of Captain Grigorovich, I have asked him to take on a more hands-on role with the men."

Mikhailovich snorted.

"Is there something amusing, sir?"

The Lieutenant General was silent for a moment. "Major Golubev does not like me very much," he said, then turned back to face Sokolov. "Tell me this: why do you think Major Golubev, with his impeccable record of service, numerous decorations, and obvious talent – why is it that he remains at the low rank of Major?"

"I can't say it has crossed my mind," Sokolov lied.

"You graduated together, have served together for decades, in army intelligence, in Afghanistan. Come now. Surely you must wonder how you, of all people, outrank Comrade Golubev. With all due respect to your distinguished career, Colonel, it has to be said that in many ways, Golubev is the outstanding soldier of his generation."

"On that we agree," Sokolov said.

"Well, then what is it? I can see nothing in his official files that would stop him from ascending to the very top. In fact, he would not be out of place commanding this entire Special Operation." He almost dared Sokolov to agree with him.

But Sokolov wasn't so stupid. He knew this topic was dangerous territory. "Well, these are not matters for a man of my rank to speculate on."

"You began your career in military intelligence, did you not?"

"I did."

"Were you ever asked to investigate Major Golubev?" Mikhailovich asked.

Sokolov thought carefully before he answered. "I have investigated many people."

"And what did you find?"

Sokolov paused again to think about his answer. "As you may have noticed, Comrade Major can have a habit of speaking beyond his station. But I assure you, he is a trusted officer of the Motherland."

Mikhailovich nodded. "Think carefully now, Colonel Sokolov. Did you ever find anything that would have the potential to compromise the Major?"

"I did not."

"Well, it just so happens I have your report into Major Golubev right here!" Mikhailovich said, picking up a folder from his desk. "Shall we read it together?"

Sokolov stiffened. "That will not be necessary, sir."

Mikhailovich was enjoying himself too much to end the matter there. He could see Sokolov's clear discomfort. He opened the folder and began to read aloud.

"'While there is some evidence to suggest that Captain Alexander Golubev has engaged in morally reprehensible social preferences and extracurricular behaviour, this investigation is unable to assert this fact to a sufficient standard of proof. It would appear Captain Golubev has been the victim of a whispering campaign designed to undermine his credibility within his division and the broader organisation.'"

He stopped briefly, looking up with a grin to see how rattled his companion was becoming before continuing. "'Furthermore, there is no evidence to suggest that Captain Golubev has been compromised by any activities or placed himself into situations that would jeopardise his own integrity or that of his post. Captain Golubev is to be cleared of these allegations, and they are to be expunged from his official record. It is recommended that Comrade Golubev receive further training regarding the risks of morally questionable social conduct.'"

Mikhailovich finished, snapping the folder shut. "What then, Comrade Colonel, do you suppose was this morally questionable social conduct?" he asked, looking at Sokolov.

Sokolov wasn't taking the bait. "Major Golubev is a fine soldier, family man and servant of the people. As you said, he was cleared of the allegations."

"And aren't you a good friend then, Comrade Colonel?"

Sokolov stood stone-faced. "I conducted the investigation without fear or favour."

"And yet you yourself found some evidence of his, and I quote, 'moral reprehensibility'."

"In my experience, envious men will say all sorts of things."

Mikhailovich raised his eyebrows. "Or perhaps you mean 'jealous'? Was a particular man jealous of Golubev? Were many men jealous of his social activities?"

Suddenly, loud explosions rang out in the night. First, at a distance. But then, getting closer.

Taking cover behind the desk, Sokolov assumed the worst and braced for potential impact. As he sat with his back to the heavy oak, he saw the look of panic on Mikhailovich's face and rolled his eyes. *A boy*, Sokolov thought to himself.

From what he could hear, it seemed to Sokolov that the new Western long-range missiles the Nativists had received had finally set their sights on their position in the city. To be honest, it had been a miracle they had been spared for this long.

Sokolov turned his mind to the nuclear plant. Surely these savages would be smart enough not to fire upon it.

But then it became clear to Sokolov what was going on. Having recognised the sounds, he smirked to himself as he slowly stood up. These were the sounds of revelry, not of revenge.

"What is it, Comrade Colonel? An attack?" said a still-cowering Mikhailovich.

Sokolov rose from his protective position. "No, sir. Look." He motioned out the window.

Slowly, Mikhailovich stood and looked for himself. On the horizon, beyond the control of the Motherland's troops, fireworks exploded into the air. Bursts of coloured light filled the night sky, like an early dawn. He looked at the horrible, evil, mocking colours. The laughing blue-and-yellow twins of his nightmares.

Mikhailovich watched in silence as the light show continued. He could sense the glee of the local Nativists in their homes. Already, he could feel their eyes on him. He could hear them whispering to one another. Discussing his failures. Laughing. Recording what they had seen via their contraband phones for the world to witness. For the East to see. For Him to see.

"'Nothing to support the intelligence', Colonel? This is your position?" Mikhailovich said, his hardened face flashing against the coloured night sky.

Sokolov's and Mikhailovich's phones buzzed with a Telegram notification. It had been sent to every device connected to the local network.

Mikhailovich opened his phone.

Happy Independence Day! We are coming home.

The sender was anonymous. Mikhailovich looked at

Sokolov with disgust before tossing his phone onto the ground with a *thud.*

* * *

Sitting in her office, Oksana received a Telegram message:

The Commander welcomes you to the Motherland and congratulates you on your Liberation. The people have registered a record "Yes" vote of 98 per cent. May peace be your guide.

Oksana's jaw immediately tightened.

The results, such as they were, had been no surprise. But this did not make it any less galling to see in black and white.

"Bastards," she said to herself.

Then, like a Christmas miracle, they had started. The explosions.

Even at this stage of the War, where everyone had grown used to the percussion of explosions and the wail of sirens, Oksana's nerves jangled slightly. But then a smile came across her face. The first real smile she'd felt in months.

She picked up the Motherland's passport sitting on her desk and tossed it into the waste bin in front of her.

It could burn.

They were coming.

CHAPTER 22

Facebook feeds read like an obituary.

Accounts of friends and family are frozen in time, never to be updated.

Across the country, the exhaustion is pervasive.

Both sides have fought to a standstill.

Two prize fighters, grappling, reaching. They sit in their corners, spent.

Help will not come for either side. It is now a question of will.

In the West, they wonder how this will end.

In the East, they claim it already has.

Total victory is prayed for. It is the only possible salvation for either side.

There must be a reckoning. From top to bottom. There

must be repentance.

But on questions of will, the answers are easy.

Do not give up on us.

This is our round.

Do not give up.

PART THREE

SPRING

CHAPTER 23

THE LONG, stubborn winter finally began to give way to spring.

The warming sun gradually broke up the frozen river, and before long the water was flowing freely once again.

Though the snow remained underfoot, it was lighter and wetter. Where there had been fresh white powder, only muck and mud remained. Though thankful for a reprieve from the cold, these brown days, void of colour, were the sort of conditions that undermine army morale even at the best of times. But when things were going badly on the battlefront, they were utterly toxic.

At the nuclear plant the work continued, but it was done more sullenly than ever. There was no danger of accident or safety breach, but beyond this absolute bare minimum of activity, there was no help given. Across the site, an old-fashioned and unspoken Union "go slow" was underway.

Across the city, particularly amongst the rank-and-file soldiers, rumours of an impending sabotage would not go away. If anything, the conspiracies compounded on themselves as the spring drew ever closer. It had been a long winter, and the men were jumpy.

In many ways one's imagination corroded the mind more than a genuine attack ever could. An explosion at the plant? A leaking of waste? A suicide bombing of the headquarters? Or worse, the barracks? These threats loomed larger than life in the mind of the Occupiers. After all, what had been successfully stopped so far? These fears, along with the scattered reports of successful Nativist counterattacks in the West and North, drove the morale of the soldiers in the town lower – if that was indeed possible.

And then there was the music. The incessant, blaring, godforsaken music.

"Have you had success in locating the source?" asked a fed-up Mikhailovich.

"We have, several times," Golubev said. "But then, of course, it starts again somewhere else."

"Do the men not know that this music, this poison to the ears, is sung by a so-called Nativist freedom fighter? A man who led the Fascist Uprising? Why, it is the music of Satan himself!" Mikhailovich snapped.

"They do," Sokolov assured him. "It is our top priority."

"Then why is it allowed to play? How is it they continue to co-opt digital networks? How are they sneaking past our sentries?"

"The men will no longer go out at night," Golubev said matter-of-factly.

Mikhailovich, who could hardly believe his ears, was immediately outraged. "What is the meaning of this breakdown in discipline? These are soldiers, not children!"

"The winter has been long. The men are exhausted and drained. Morale is low," Golubev calmly replied.

"And what of *my* morale? I cannot sleep with this noise! This evil noise haunts my dreams and my waking hours." His hands clenched into tight fights.

"Perhaps we could let the men take leave, or request reinforcements from the East," Sokolov suggested. While trying to be helpful, he understood these options were completely unrealistic.

"Or perhaps we could consider importing creature comforts such as drink, or better food. Or women," said Golubev.

"Are you both to suggest that I call East and ask for deliveries of food, booze and whores? Are we planning an orgy that I don't know of, Comrade Major?" Mikhailovich said with disgust. "No. You will order the men out, and they will patrol. And if they do not, you will arrest them. And if they resist, you will shoot them." Mikhailovich's breathing was becoming slightly laboured as he pointed his finger at Golubev with a hint of uncontrolled menace.

Golubev looked at Sokolov for help.

"The men are scared, sir," Sokolov said finally.

"*Scared*?"

"Yes," answered Sokolov.

"They fear sabotage," said Golubev, backing up his friend.

"Well, tell them there is no sabotage to be feared. Tell them it is Nativist propaganda," Mikhailovich said with a tone that feigned to sound reasonable.

"Well, Comrade Lieutenant General, the men believe the intelligence," said Golubev.

"They trust their leader's *judgment* of the intelligence. After all, we have been pursuing a Fascist plot for the entire winter," said Sokolov.

Mikhailovich narrowed his eyes and rubbed his face. "Yes. Of course." He paused briefly. "But we must maintain discipline. We simply cannot have this bunker mentality take hold. The Nativists and the Fascists will come to believe that we are weak."

Golubev raised his eyebrows. "There are limits to what men will do. Even under orders."

"Perhaps *your* orders. Perhaps it is your weakness they feed on, Major," said Mikhailovich, pointing his finger. "The men will do what they are told."

"Then perhaps you would like to tell them yourself?" Golubev said. "I am sure they would appreciate an address from the Lieutenant General. Perhaps you are right. Perhaps it is me."

"They will do as I tell them, I assure you," said Mikhailovich, glaring.

"Men follow where they are led. Not where they are told," said Golubev.

"Excuses, excuses. Nothing but excuses and cowardice from you, Comrade Major!" said Mikhailovich. He began slowly and carefully pacing the room.

"Cowardice? It is one thing to witness fighting, sir. It is another to order fighting, to know that those men will die. It is another thing, yet again, to fight and kill oneself. And once one has seen it, once one has done it, one never lusts for it again," Golubev said.

"It is your moral incorrigibility that they see. They will only follow a *real* man, not one who would rather dance with them," Mikhailovich said, sneering. "Or shower."

Golubev looked at Sokolov. His friend gently shook his head, pleading with Golubev to tread lightly.

"And what do you know of morality?" said Golubev.

"Enough to know that men like you brought about the downfall of the Empire. Men of weakness. Men who could not stand up for what was right when it was most needed. Men who brought down the Wall and let evil and moral bankruptcy in. And look what your cowardly weakness has given us."

Golubev shook his head. "This Empire you lust for, it's a figment of your dreams."

Mikhailovich's mouth began to twitch, his face filled with scarlet. "*You* will see. *They* will see!" he spat, pointing out the window in the dark. "Those who prostituted my country and our women. Those who stole and enriched themselves while the people suffered. They will pay. They will all pay – and they are! We are rebuilding and reclaiming what is rightfully the property of the Motherland. What those West would seek to take for themselves in collaboration with the Nativist Fascists, we have taken back for her glory. No, this humiliation that you and your kind enabled, it is at an end once and for all!"

Golubev did not respond. There was nothing to be said.

The Lieutenant General took a moment to compose himself. "But, thankfully you and the men needn't worry. I have obtained important information from inside the enemy camp that will put this Fascist plot to an end once and for all." He said this all in a pleasant, flat tone.

"And might I ask, sir, who is in charge of this investigation?" asked Sokolov.

Mikhailovich smiled. "You needn't worry, my dear Comrade Colonel. The matter is well in hand. Like a lamppost in the evening, it is casting light in the darkest corners."

* * *

Outside the Administration building, the early spring evening was quietly percolating with post-winter life. Encouraged by the warmer weather and first green shoots, locals were outside for the first time in months. Even a few tea houses had chosen to stay open later than usual to take advantage of the foot traffic. It was almost as though life had returned to the streets of Heryvin.

Suddenly, the silence of the evening was broken as a loud and shaking explosion rang through the air. The loud bang couldn't just be heard by those in the room. It could be felt. The sort of explosion that shakes one's bone marrow.

Sokolov and Golubev instantly knew – this was close. It was from inside the city limits, without question.

Sirens began to wail in the dark. Radios barked information. Soldier patrols in jeeps, trucks and vans swarmed on the scene.

"The dam, get to the dam!"

"Confirmed explosion at the dam!"

"Emergency crews on the way!"

It had been several minutes before Mikhailovich, Golubev and Sokolov arrived on the scene. The drive to the industrial park had been quick, but taken in a tight and tense silence. All three men were contemplating what lay ahead of them in the darkness and what it would mean.

Mikhailovich breathed a sigh of relief. He had feared the

worst as the jeep sped along the winding asphalt road to the industrial park. In the darkness of the night, Mikhailovich's mind had raced with all the potential evils the Nativists could inflict upon him. Had they finally poisoned the river water, as he feared? Had they damaged the dam and canal infrastructure?

They pulled up to the industrial park. Mercifully, the dam was intact.

But the river itself was another story entirely. It was still flowing with water. But something was different.

Mikhailovich struggled to see in the dark exactly what the situation was, but his heart began racing with panic. What had happened? And why was the water moving in that peculiar and unnatural way? What had these animals done?

Downstream, a curious crowd was gathered on the ridge of the riverbank. Silhouettes of people gathered were clearly pointing down into the water. They could see it too.

Mikhailovich ordered the search lights to be pointed onto the river. Or what could be seen of it, given the late hour.

Down on the embankment, Golubev reached into the water and scooped out several of the floating objects that had blanketed the surface of the water. Smooth. Plastic. Recognisable. But what were they?

Golubev pulled his phone from his pocket and hit the flashlight button.

In the darkness, Sokolov could hear Golubev laughing. "Sasha?" he called out. The Colonel walked semi-blindly into the darkness of the evening, guided by the sound of the river and the chuckling laughter of his friend.

Finally locating the shaking silhouette of the chuckling Golubev, Sokolov was about to ask him what on earth he was carrying on about when he saw for himself.

"Bath time!" said Golubev, tossing one of the small plastic objects to Sokolov.

The soft plastic object squeaked as Sokolov caught it. A rubber ducky. Yellow, naturally. He didn't need to look to guess the colour of the other one Golubev was juggling happily in his hands.

Sokolov turned the duck over in his hand as he studied it closely. A message was written underneath.

People of the Southern Peninsula, we love you! And we are coming!

Sokolov shook his head and smirked at the ridiculousness of the entire enterprise.

Intelligence just wasn't what it used to be.

CHAPTER 24

EVERY NIGHT the signs go up around the city.

The faster they are taken down, the faster they go back up.

Nobody is seen putting them up. The source? Never found. Magic.

Emblazoned next to images of victorious Nativist soldiers carrying advanced weaponry are the following words:

"Occupiers, we know who you are.

Your armies are failing.

You are losing. And we are nearing.

The enemy is reminded for every atrocity committed: the looting, killing, rape and destruction – you will be held to account. You will pay.

Let's stand up for our defenders.

Let's keep the stretch going!

We believe in the Armed Forces of the Homeland!

Glory to the Heroes!"

The signs send chills down the spines of the Occupiers. Because they can feel the net tightening too.

We are coming.

You may stay, though you will only stay in vain.

You may run, though you will not run far.

The truth will follow you.

As will we.

We are coming.

We are coming home.

CHAPTER 25

OLEKSANDR SAT ALONE in the dark, drinking from a cheap bottle of Motherland vodka.

In his left hand he held a rubber ducky. It smiled at him. He had managed to salvage a blue one during the clean-up after the incident.

These rubber duckies were a hot item, and Oleksandr knew that despite the very clear instructions for every duck to be destroyed, most people in town had squirrelled away at least a few. No doubt members of the Great Rubber Armada would one day become historic souvenirs.

But when? When would this madness end? The thought that it might go forever depressed Oleksandr. Even now, in this moment, he deplored the death and the violence.

He thought about exacting revenge on Mikhailovich,

but that would be like shooting a dog for hunting. This was not what they had agreed to when they first spoke under the lamppost several weeks ago. Mikhailovich had assured him that while there might be arrests, nobody would be harmed.

There was nobody to blame but himself. That was the only truth that remained. Even though Oleksandr had done the wrong thing for the right reasons, that made him no less guilty of treason.

"Traitor," Oleksandr said to himself while throwing the small rubber duck onto the ground with a *thunk*. "That's how they'll remember you."

After the release of the ducks, there had been a frantic effort from the Occupiers to stop the flow of the little rubber heroes that night and into the next day.

Nets were placed in the water.

Soldiers scooped with their hands.

Improvised barrier devices were erected.

Here was The Commander's Great Army, on its literal knees, trying to collect children's toys. This was what it had come to.

With straight faces, the Occupiers claimed their efforts had succeeded. But Oleksandr had already heard reports of blue and yellow messages of love floating into the Peninsula port and other small inlets located along the way. The cover of darkness, the rapid flow of the melting river – not to mention the sheer number of the bobbing and weaving birds – ensured the success of the cunning plan.

Inevitably, images of the bobbing ducks were appearing across messenger channels and international news outlets.

Rubber duckies. They'd made it through where others couldn't.

He had to admit it was an idea brilliant in its simplicity, creativity and audaciousness.

But how had she managed to get so many of them?

To Oleksandr, it wasn't the idea that mattered. It was her. Somehow, he'd overlooked what was so obvious to everyone else. She really was a brilliant, natural leader. Even at her age.

Picking up the blue rubber ducky from the ground, Oleksandr held it in his hand up to the weak light of the moon. *Such a silly thing*, he thought. *Such a silly, troublesome thing*.

Before the Invasion, Oleksandr could never have imagined that such an innocent object could cause such trouble. But who could have imagined any of this?

When he'd first heard of the most recent stunt, he couldn't help but feel relieved. With behaviour escalating on both sides and tensions high, Oleksandr had become convinced that someone was about to do something irrevocably insane. The constant hounding by the military police about a plot involving the city's river and water supplies couldn't have been for nothing. The stress of the action itself, as well as the inevitable reprisals, was keeping him up at night. He couldn't compromise the safety of his people, not again.

So then why had the truth of it – the actual truth – not

been obvious to him? When he'd first detected the outsized order as part of his routine duties at the plant, Oleksandr naturally assumed it was for the chemicals listed. He didn't know it had been a code, hidden in plain sight for someone in the know to ferry outside of the plant.

And the reference to ducks? Well, anyone worth his salt understood the language of the gulags. He'd wrongly believed the Occupiers had Collaborators on the inside that were going to set them all on the course to ruin. That was why he had to raise the alarm.

Oleksandr knew he could never convince his own side not to do it. Ideologues can never be persuaded from a course of action. Had he raised it with the partisans, they'd have just shifted their strategy to something else while freezing him out entirely.

So, he had no choice but to tell the Invaders about the plot. This wasn't ratting or breaking the Union code. This was about stopping a disaster.

But everyone was wrong, including him. *Especially* him. There were no vats of poison, no burning rivers or explosive sabotage, just harmless children's toys. She was so brilliant that she hid her creative innocence in broad daylight. But they couldn't see it. Instead, corrupted people like Mikhailovich or those hard of head like Oleksdandr assumed the worst of the world.

But even so, why had they done it? Why did they need

to provoke? Surely, these so-called patriots realised the danger they were putting everyone in? Surely, she knew her luck would run out?

Everyone has a limit. Especially men like him.

Oleksandr squeezed the rubber tightly. The squeaking sound took him back to his memories of the girl. *She always loved her rubber duckies*, Oleksandr thought to himself with a smile. But why hadn't anyone told him? Why hadn't *she* told him? After all these years, she couldn't trust him? That's what hurt the most: the lack of trust. Why didn't she come to him?

But who was he to lecture on trust? He had been the one to break the code of honour, not her. He spoke. He put them in danger.

She made her choice, and so did he.

Oleksandr took another large swig from the bottle. The liquid burned as he gulped it down. He burped loudly, the sound echoing in the empty square of the city centre.

Looking inside the now-empty bottle, a slightly drunken Oleksandr tapped at the base, hoping to find a few last drops inside. Defeated, he tapped the bottle against his forehead and gently sobbed a little.

This was the first time he had cried in . . . well, he couldn't remember when. Maybe The Accident.

"Pathetic," he sobbed quietly. "Pathetic."

In a flash of pain and anger, Oleksandr threw the empty bottle violently against the ground. The smash echoed loudly as the bottle shattered. With nothing left to break, Oleksandr screamed primordially into the void of the dark night before slumping onto the ground.

He couldn't stop playing it over and over in his head. How had this happened?

Had he known the truth, Oleksandr was sure he'd have done things differently. Maybe he could have warned her. Maybe he could have saved her.

Maybe.

For Oleksandr, the days since the ducks flooded the river had been a blur. He'd desperately wanted to take it all back.

If only Elena hadn't got involved, putting ideas in her head. It was possible he could have still fixed it.

But now? He'd never know. She was gone. They were both gone.

Oleksandr had given up the "intelligence" to Mikhailovich, and it had cost him everything. For the first and only time in his life, Oleksandr had broken the one thing he truly believed in: unity.

He had been a fool to trust a madman like Mikhailovich. Oleksandr knew he should have listened to Sasha when he told him the Lieutenant General was not like the leaders they'd both served under in the Empire. Golubev had told him that this was a man without honour. But because he was certain he was stopping a catastrophe, the old fool had done it anyway.

But, of course, she was too clever to do anything truly

evil, like everyone was assuming. Her heart was too loving for her people and her country. But why hadn't she told him?

Perhaps it didn't matter. For his own selfish martyrdom, Oleksandr was prepared to throw a brave stranger to a wolf like Mikhailovich.

Would he have felt so guilty had it not been her? Or would he have gone on living without a care? Oleksandr, if he was being entirely truthful, didn't know the answer to that question. And it made him feel sick.

And now, thanks to her unbreakable silence, Oleksandr's loose lips had cost the lives of two people he loved.

That was the undeniable truth.

As the moon came out from behind the clouds, Oleksandr noticed the two shadows looming over him.

It's time, he thought to himself.

Oleksandr closed his eyes and waited for it to come.

"Please forgive me, my darlings," Oleksandr sobbed.

He tried to do the right thing.

He tried to stop the madness.

And no good deed goes unpunished.

"Murderer," Oleksandr said to himself.

* * *

When the search lights had come on and the men had swarmed, nobody was more surprised at what he found than

Mikhailovich.

Surely this could not be the one they were after. *How could she possibly be the mastermind behind all of these events?* Mikhailovich thought.

But the intelligence from his source had been clear.

And, it was a very, very good source. Mikhailovich had turned one of their own against them, and he loved it.

This, he had been told, was where the Fascist cell was bringing in the contraband. Hidden through the routine orders of the nuclear facility, the Fascists were moving large quantities of materials in and out of the city. Even if he didn't intercept the chemical delivery, Mikhailovich was confident he could majorly disrupt the cell's operations.

If the intelligence was indeed correct – and so far, it had been good – then Mikhailovich could cut the head of the Fascist snake in an instant.

And there she was, located at the now-tainted drop-off point. Waiting for the intercepted goods that were not coming.

It had to be her.

In any event, it didn't matter. He'd apprehended a Fascist, and she could lead him to the others. Even if she wasn't *The* Fascist, this was still a breakthrough worth celebrating.

One thing Mikhailovich knew for certain was that she did have links to the Union. This was beyond doubt, and this he would easily prove. And then, with those links proven, Mikhailovich would have his prize. And his sweet, cold revenge.

He was pleased. Finally, some good news.

This would be fun.

* * *

Looking at the assembled brief of evidence and assorted items on his desk, Mikhailovich considered that perhaps she was the Fascist leader after all.

"You must give her a trial," said Golubev, miserable when he saw the prisoner and knew exactly who she was. *Whose* she was. "Justice must at least be seen to be done."

An orderly trial with the gathering of evidence would slow matters down, cool hot tempers or perhaps let new leadership arrive from the East – at least, that's what Golubev hoped. Surely, his superiors back home knew what was happening here. Surely, he thought to himself in vain.

Mikhailovich rolled his eyes while tossing a yellow rubber ducky in the air.

"She's of no importance," Sokolov offered. "Let's hold her and keep squeezing; she'll crack if she knows anything. In the end, they always do. Trust me, sir. Let me keep digging. We'll get to the bottom of this." He was trying his hardest to back up Golubev with a strategy that might be more appealing to Mikhailovich's sensibilities.

Any of these options might have been possible before the searches began. But then the supporting intelligence was gathered.

Maps.

Lists.

Dozens of burner phones.

The original video of the Final Sunrise taken from Sokolov's office.

Yellow and blue paint.

Fireworks.

A crate of rubber duckies.

Flag pins.

"Look at all of this," Mikhailovich said, waving his arm over the sample of items collected. "Tell me, how is this not the Fascist Cell leader? I'll be honest, I didn't believe it myself when we first arrested her. I was even a little disappointed, given my suspicions. But as far as I am concerned, this is open and shut. She is a terrorist, responsible for an ongoing and increasing campaign of sabotage against the Motherland and must be treated accordingly."

"Abramovich doesn't think she did it," Golubev ventured.

Mikhailovich laughed at the delicious irony. "Tell Oleksandr Abramovich he will be a guest of honour at the ceremony. After all, we couldn't have done it without him. He told me he wanted to save lives. Well, he has. He has given us a terrorist mastermind who had been plotting to destroy this entire city! And you both know what the punishment for terror is, especially in this newly designated jurisdiction of the

Motherland." Mikhailovich chuckled at the thought.

Golubev and Sokolov looked at one another. Under the Motherland's laws, terrorists could be put to death if it was in the defence of the Motherland or her people.

"She is no mastermind. And besides – so far, we only have evidence of her defacing a statue, painting messages on buildings, setting off fireworks and unleashing rubber duckies. As egregious as these are, none are capital offences," Golubev said, looking to Sokolov for help.

"Perhaps she is merely a lieutenant for the broader cell, sir. We need her alive to continue our efforts to destroy them," Sokolov said.

Mikhailovich smiled and shook his head. From inside his jacket pocket, he revealed a small bottle of clear liquid.

"What's this?" Golubev asked.

"This, Comrade Major, is the final piece of the puzzle," Mikhailovich said, holding the bottle between his forefinger and thumb. "This is the poison that killed Grigorovich." He placed the bottle on the table next to the other assembled items with a loud *clunk*. "It was found at the school this morning."

Golubev looked to Sokolov in desperation. This was insane.

"And who conducted this search, sir?" Sokolov asked a little desperately.

"This is not your concern."

"Well, we should run the appropriate laboratory tests and

then interrogate the suspect as to where she sourced the material. Perhaps she will lead us to more targets," Sokolov said.

"Well, should we at least ask her if it is hers?" Golubev said.

"Ha! And have her deny it? Tell me, what has she said thus far? Has she not claimed to have acted alone? Has she not refused to tell us the name of any accomplices? Well, I am of the view we simply must take her at her word!" Mikhailovich said.

"Yes, but neither of us believes what she is saying. It's obvious she can only be an underling. Isn't that right, Comrade Colonel?" Golubev said.

Sokolov didn't respond. He could see where this was going. It was too late.

"You gentle, gentle men. No wonder the Empire collapsed on your watch. As you know, an enemy of the people must be dealt with, especially one who has executed such lethal intent against the Motherland. Think of poor Captain Grigorovich and his family! Surely you agree we must honour his memory and bring his killer to justice.

"But never you mind, there's no need for your squeamishness. This is my decision alone, and as the ranking officer on this mission, I am comfortable in making it," Mikhailovich said.

For the Lieutenant General, there was only one way to deal with a Fascist murderer: strike the shepherd to scatter the sheep.

A message must be sent to others who wished the Motherland harm. And it would be sent.

"She will hang," Mikhailovich told a stunned Golubev and Sokolov.

* * *

Oksana found Oleksandr's body in the early morning light, the gun still in his hand.

His body was slumped forward in the middle of Union Square, with dark blood running down his face and onto his blue overalls.

Above his body was Katya's. His granddaughter's shoes swung gently in the morning breeze.

And next to Katya's shoes were Elena's.

Elena, who had come to beg Mikhailovich for her student's young life. Elena, who had tried to fix it all by claiming Katya's work as her own. She had been punished too.

There they were. Student and teacher, side by side. Just as Elena had promised.

And under them both, a heartbroken grandfather and devoted friend.

The tragedy was too much for Oksana to bear. She fell to her knees and sobbed.

For his part, Mikhailovich had believed Elena when she said it was all her doing. He knew the Fascists were coordinating.

He just didn't think it was in the high schools. But now, thanks to Elena, Mikhailovich had all the proof he needed.

"An added bonus," Mikhailovich boasted on the telephone to his superiors back East. "Two Fascists for the price of one!"

He couldn't believe his luck. Spring was coming at last.

CHAPTER 26

IT SMELLS OF SPRING.

The sun is rising.

Hope is growing.

The Reaper snarls.

Like a tide going out, his evil begins to recede.

Pushed back at first. Now flooding backwards.

Munitions dumps are destroyed behind enemy lines. Logistics are disrupted. Bridges are blown. Entire jet divisions are vaporised.

The training is working. The determination paying dividends. The unthinkable is now thinkable.

Gradually, the enemy is being expelled or surrounded.

As the Occupiers leave their forward positions, they sabotage and destroy the railways and roads. Those heading East, naturally.

And the evidence. They must destroy the evidence.
But the world has seen.
It watches Heroes fighting.
What happens there matters here. It matters everywhere.
And in the warm spring sun, the cherry blossoms bloom.
The dark is giving way to the light.
The people are prevailing.
Their glory is reflected to the world.
For liberty. For justice. For humanity.
They are coming home.

CHAPTER 27

Oksana stood in the middle of the windswept Union Square holding the coloured bundle in her arms.

She was alone. On the ground next to her was a set of large, industrial bolt cutters.

The Occupier soldiers on duty watched her warily from the distance. Given she was by herself, she presented no major threat, they reasoned. So they did nothing.

Oksana ignored them. She no longer cared; they could kill her too. No matter what happened, she would not leave her three friends like this.

But she needn't have worried. The soldiers were the ones who were afraid.

Oksana had watched the evil event happen the night before. Ritualistic murder with a legalistic veneer. It sickened her. And though she was powerless to stop it, she could not leave Elena and Katya to face their awful fate on their own. Even the very thought of them alone and scared brought tears to Oksana's eyes. She simply had to be there. And so, in the dark and rainy night, Oksana stood and bore witness to their bravery.

Together they were marched out. Katya first. Then Elena.

Dressed in grey jumpsuits, both had their heads covered with black bags, the kind Oksana immediately recognised. Their hands were bound behind their backs. Only their respective heights – Katya tall and lean, Elena small and rakish – gave them away.

Both were told to stand in front of the hastily constructed wooden gallows.

Then the bags came off. The fresh rain felt cool on their faces.

Though they were both afraid, Katya and Elena were determined not to show it. They had agreed in private conversations that they would resist to the end. It was all they had, and they were determined to cling to it.

They were heroes, Oksana thought to herself.

A thick, nylon-roped noose was placed over Katya's head and tightened around her neck. She stared ahead, refusing to show any emotion.

Then it was Elena's turn.

At gunpoint, they were forced onto the stools in front of them.

They stood proudly.

Katya, demonstrating bravery, honour and dignity beyond her years, had accepted her fate. The precocious young talent had long been ready to die for her country. And now she would.

For her part, Elena had no regrets. She would not lose another child to war – she would stand beside her beautiful pupil, just as she had promised. And heroes must never die alone.

Elena looked at Katya and smiled. Even without her glasses on, Katya's incredible strength of character beamed back and warmed her soul. For the first time in a long time, she was at peace.

"Glory to the Homeland," Katya had said.

"Glory to the Heroes," Elena had replied.

Closing her eyes, Elena whispered to herself, believing the words that left her lips never more than she did at that moment: "The sun will rise again."

Then the stools were kicked.

And then they kicked.

And then it was over.

The awful moment, a fleeting second that lasted an eternity.

The rain fell silently as the executioners walked back into their headquarters. Oksana looked away. Raindrops mingled with the tears rolling down her cheeks.

In the distance, she saw Oleksandr standing with his

hands in his pockets. His head was dropped. The poor man had just witnessed the murder of his only granddaughter, along with an old friend.

Oksana wanted to run to him, to hug him. She wanted to hug everyone, and kill the Invaders, and end the madness of this War.

As Oleksandr raised his head, his eyes met Oksana's, empty and vacant. As she watched him walk away, somehow she knew it would be the last time she ever saw him.

* * *

Sokolov was in his office, drinking coffee, smoking, watching the sunrise. He had been watching the Union leader go about her business since before dawn.

Whatever she was up to, he didn't care. Even a few days ago, he'd have ordered the men to stop her. But it hardly seemed to matter now. They didn't want to do it, and he wasn't going to force them.

He'd spent the morning reading the latest military reports from the frontline and studying maps of the area surrounding the city. It was only a matter of time. Based on his understanding of deployments and topography, Sokolov calculated that the Motherland's Western divisions could slow the enemy's advance for a day or two at most. After that, the Nativists would be in the city.

It was all guesswork, but Sokolov was sure of this: he wasn't going to die. This was one promise he intended to keep. To hell with Mikhailovich.

He wandered to the window, peering out at the square. He watched as Oksana approached the young Fascist's body first. She stood on a ladder, cutting her down gently. Sokolov was surprised at how easily Oksana managed to hold, then lower Katya's body to the ground. What impossible strength was she drawing on?

On the fringes of the square, he could see his men scurrying about. Like busy ants, they were packing trucks with whatever they could lay their hands on. Word about the situation on the fringes of the city had obviously gone around, and panic was taking hold.

Though the military fallback would need to be orderly to preserve the integrity of the army's lines, Sokolov knew it wouldn't be. Losing a war is messy at the best of times, and the men had lost their nerve weeks ago. This would be a disorderly, dishonourable retreat.

Studying the scene unfolding on the ground, Sokolov revised his previous prediction to less than a day. Maybe hours. It was time to get moving.

A loud voice broke his concentration.

"And what is the meaning of this?" barked Mikhailovich from the doorway.

"The meaning of what?" Sokolov asked without breaking

his stance. He was tired of Mikhailovich and his self-aggrandising nonsense.

Mikhailovich stormed into the room and approached the panoramic window.

"I gave clear orders that these Fascists were to hang for a week!" he roared, pointing outside.

Sokolov exhaled loudly. "Orders . . ."

"Yes, you remember what those are, don't you, Comrade Colonel? I am still in command of this Special Operation."

"For the next few hours, certainly," Sokolov said, drawing on his cigarette.

"Surely you do not believe this propogandist nonsense from the Nativists and their Western sponsors. These reports of retreat are false, Comrade Colonel. Our lines hold. Our armies are preparing to attack this very instant. This so-called Fascist counterattack will fail, and victory will be ours!"

Sokolov snorted at Mikhailovich's delusions. It was time to set this petulant child straight. "Our reports have the Nativists approaching the city limits. The bridges crossing the river to the east of our position have already been destroyed by their long-range strike capabilities and saboteurs, making our exits challenging at best."

He paused to put the cigarette to his lips and blew out a billow of smoke before he continued. "We must give up our position here and fall back into the Eastern Independent Republics. Perhaps we can regroup our collective lines there. If we remain in the city, we will be cut off and eventually captured. Or worse. There is nothing further to be gained in staying," Sokolov concluded, smoke still coming from his nostrils.

"Give up our position? And what of our mission objectives? Have you forgotten the Motherland? Have you forgotten the people of the Peninsula? And what will happen to them should this river be blocked once again? Your selfishness is despicable, Comrade Colonel," Mikhailovich said.

Golubev entered the room and immediately sensed the tension in the air. He'd come to see Sokolov in his office for a private conversation and had not expected to run into Mikhailovich. In fact, Mikhailovich's leadership was the very topic he had wanted to discuss.

"Oh, Major Golubev, I see you've finally chosen to grace us with your presence. Can you explain to me how this can be allowed?" Mikhailovich said, gesturing dismissively out the window.

"And what is it I am allowing, sir?" Golubev asked.

"You have been on the streets, Golubev?" asked Mikhailovich impatiently.

"Yes, sir."

"Well then, tell me. What is the meaning of this?"

"Of what?" Golubev didn't have time for this nonsense. None of them did.

"Of this Fascista outside! Tell me, how is it she is allowed to move around uninhibited and violate my very clear orders?

As I have repeatedly instructed you, those bodies were to hang for a week!"

Golubev was silent.

"Major, you are to radio and order your men to fire upon Oksana Shevchenko this very instant. She is a terrorist and is currently performing an illegal operation endangering the Motherland's security."

Golubev sighed. "The men have lost confidence, Lieutenant General. There has been a collapse in discipline."

"Perhaps it is *you* who has lost confidence, Comrade Major."

Golubev sniffed his disgust.

"What you do not realise, my dear gentlemen, is that the men have not yet heard our latest orders. They will be as heartened as I am once they do," said Mikhailovich with a grin that surprised both Golubev and Sokolov.

"Latest orders?" Golubev couldn't help himself.

"As you both would be aware, the Motherland has not yet begun to scratch the surface of her true military capability. She has held back her most devastating weaponry from this fight. Despite the bad manners of the Nativists, we have chosen to be neighbourly. But, our understanding is at an end . . ."

Sokolov and Golubev exchanged an uneasy glance. Surely it had not come to that. Not even in the darkest moments of the Empire had anyone truly contemplated launching the unthinkable.

"Now, regrettably, while those in the East have not yet reached the threshold of offensive annihilation, we *do* have strategically significant defensive assets at our disposal in this very city," said Mikhailovich. "These are capabilities that, if creatively harnessed, can help turn the tide of this battle in our favour."

While Golubev and Sokolov felt slightly relieved – there would be no Armageddon – both men were still wary of where Mikhailovich was going.

"This morning I received word that we are to utilise the nuclear plant for maximum deterrence and, if necessary, maximum impact," Mikhailovich said.

"'Maximum deterrence'?" asked Golubev, his blood running cold.

"Think, Comrade Major. You are not entirely daft. We have a nuclear facility at our disposal, do we not?" Mikhailovich pointed to the nuclear plant in the distance. "This facility can be switched from neutral to defence, and from defence to offence with relative ease. Why, with a few tweaks, she can be made a part of the Motherland's great military umbrella."

Golubev turned ashen. "Surely you cannot mean—"

"And, if the worst should happen," said Mikhailovich, cutting off Golubev before he could continue, "I have intelligence in my possession indicating the Fascists intend to attack our disclosed defensive positions at the nuclear plant and then *blame* us for the wreckage! Can you imagine such recklessness?

Attacking a nuclear facility of this size? It would be for the Fascists to explain how this disaster unfolded as part of their ill-founded attacks on our freely Liberated people."

"A false flag," said Sokolov. His years of intelligence experience helped him to decipher the Machiavellian plotting and nonsense of Mikhailovich's rambling. The Lieutenant General was so unhinged, he was prepared to attack a nuclear power plant and then falsely accuse the other side of being behind it.

Mikhailovich laughed. "Wheels within wheels, Colonel. Wheels within wheels."

"And what of the costs?" Golubev asked.

"Well, they are accustomed to accidents of that nature here, are they not? It will be no great loss."

Golubev shook his head. He couldn't believe his ears. This was madness. Utter madness.

"Very well, sir," Sokolov said. "Would you be prepared to share these orders and the associated intelligence so that we can make the appropriate preparations? The men will need to be properly briefed."

"It is for my eyes only, I'm afraid," said Mikhailovich.

Sokolov looked at Golubev.

"But of course, sir, I understand. Do not fear, it will be done. Major Golubev will handle Miss Shevchenko. I will ensure the plant is prepared, per the emergency protocols. We will send our artillery and defensive units to the plant and instruct them to dig in accordingly."

"Be sure that you do," said Mikhailovich, satisfied with what he heard.

Outside the office both Sokolov and Golubev agreed. To hell with the supposed orders.

It was time to leave. One way or another.

* * *

In the square, Oksana had cut down both Katya and Elena.

The three bodies now lay on the cold, wet concrete in a neat row with their arms crossed on their chests. Katya was in the middle. Given her connection to both Elena and Oleksandr, this seemed the most appropriate way to let the three of them rest for now.

Oksana surveyed the tragic sight. Her heart wept. But despite the danger in doing this under the watchful eyes of the Invaders, she was determined to give the three of them peace. No matter what, she would honour these fallen heroes.

She unbundled the items in her arms. Carefully she laid out the four flags in front of her. The richness of the blue silk panel and the brightness of the yellow underneath caught her eyes. The morning sun, which had broken through the clouds, seemed to make them glow more brightly.

Oksana held the smooth fabric in her hands, running it between her fingers.

Colours, Oksana thought to herself. *Such curious things.*

Meaningless, really, until given meaning. And then, suddenly, worth dying for.

She had ached for the sight of this unique combination of colour. But she hadn't realised how much her eyes had missed catching glimpses of these emblems in everyday life until she saw them once again. With everything that had happened, Oksana could literally feel the colours flowing from the fabric and into her soul. She felt warm. Whole.

Deliberately and carefully, Oksana walked forward, holding one of the flags in her hand. She placed it over Katya. A young hero, who did not die in vain. Now draped in the colours of her people, she could finally rest.

Oksana picked up the second. She placed it over Elena. Though her heart broke, Oksana understood why Elena had done it. She wished she'd taken Elena's place. She wished she could be so giving, so selfless. Elena had always been giving and selfless, even in death. *That was her*, Oksana thought to herself. The principal was now at rest. She was back with her family and with the many children whose lives she had touched.

The third flag was for Oleksandr. Oksana stood over him with the flag in her hands. She could only hope that this good man, this all too decent man, had found comfort from his pain. No matter his actions, Oksana knew Olek's heart was pure. He wished harm to none and peace to all. Laying down the flag, Oksana promised the old man he would now have it.

She took a step backwards, surveying the three heroes

draped in the colours of the Homeland.

Suddenly, the words came to her. These were words she hadn't thought of since high school, when Elena had first taught her the deeds of the original freedom fighters.

One legendary scholar and poet had always spoken to Oksana. A man by the name of Shevchenko, he was Elena's favourite too.

And so, like an ancient hymn, Oksana recited the poetry of her country.

"When I die,
let me rest, let me lie
amidst our Homeland's broad steppes.
Let me see
the endless fields and steep slopes I hold so dear.
Let me hear our river's great roar."

A tear rolled down Oksana's cheek as she finished. In the distance, the fighting and explosions were moving closer to the city.

It was time.

They were coming.

* * *

One only had to listen to sounds to know the fighting was fierce. It was also getting closer.

The explosions were now on the outskirts of the city. The rumble of each exploding shell and bomb could be felt reverberating through the city roads and its buildings.

The local people were inside, watching from their windows and on their contraband phones. Posting what they could see to the world. Sharing data points with the advancing Heroes about what they knew.

The dogs barked from the deafening noise, but it was the Motherland soldiers who were panicked.

For the last hour, Sokolov and Golubev had flatly refused to convey Mikhailovich's orders. Technically this wasn't insubordination or a breach of command. It was just slow. They'd get to it. Eventually. From the street corner by the Administration building, they listened to the sound of war quickly approaching.

"Ten miles," Golubev said.

Sokolov nodded and exhaled his cigarette. "Moving fast," he replied calmly.

A fresh explosion surged through the ground, knocking over a planted pot a few metres away.

Golubev looked at the smashed crockery and smirked. "Maybe nine," he said.

Sokolov lit another cigarette. He had a good chain going as he dropped the latest butt on the ground.

"I don't know how you're not dead," said Golubev, shaking his head.

Sokolov laughed. "Well, there's still time yet!"

Golubev smiled. Gallows humour was about all they had left at this point. "And you are leaving?" he asked his comrade.

Sokolov nodded. "It makes no sense to stay here and to die."

"And what will you do back East?"

"What I've always done. What else is there to do?" Sokolov said, somewhat surprised.

"I can't continue like this. I can't go back," Golubev said, putting his hands into his pockets.

"But where else is there to go? A man of your record cannot go West, cannot stay here. There's only the Motherland. Despite everything, you will be protected there."

"After what has happened here? After what we have done to this place? And worse elsewhere. How can we go back? How can we hold our heads high?"

Sokolov took a long draw of his cigarette. "It's the job. That's all it is."

"There is no honour here," Golubev said, looking at the ground.

"Only war," Sokolov said, exhaling smoke into the air. "We can only knock off the edges. That's all we can do." Out of the corner of his eye, he saw a figure walking briskly toward them.

"And what is the meaning of this?" Mikhailovich roared as he gestured toward the street.

Panicked soldiers were filling trucks and cars they'd

commandeered from the locals.

Not waiting for orders, some desperate men had already started to leave.

"Of what?" asked Sokolov, amidst the chaos.

"Of this insubordination!"

"But our lines hold, do they not? What is the sense of urgency, Comrade Lieutenant General?" Golubev replied with a smile.

"Careful in your tone, Golubev. I will have you court-marshalled for this! And this time, he won't be able to cover for you." He turned to Sokolov. "And what of the nuclear plant? What has been done with the protocols? Have the cooling stations been switched off? Have the fuel rods been moved into position?"

"A work in progress, sir," Sokolov said, stamping out his cigarette.

Mikhailovich looked at Sokolov with contempt. "You have no idea what it is to win a war." He shook his head. "No matter. There are ways to destroy those in quick time. Your impertinence is meaningless."

A solider walking past caught Mikhailovich's eye. "You, there, Captain Semenov!" Mikhailovich yelled at the fresh-faced soldier with dark, cropped black hair and thickish build, carting what was clearly a looted washing machine on a dolly.

The young man set the load aside and walked over sheepishly. "For my girlfriend . . ." he explained, his face reddening.

"Captain – sorry, should I say, *Colonel* Semenov. You seem like a man of talent," Mikhailovich said.

"Thank you, sir," said Semenov, a tremor in his voice. The young man could feel the tension between his three commanding officers.

"You have been responsible for managing our artillery defences, have you not?" Mikhailovich asked.

"Yes. I mean, sometimes. Well, not really. No, sir," stammered Semenov.

Sokolov chuckled to himself.

"But you know how to use it, do you not? You are a trained solider, yes?" Mikhailovich barked.

"Yes. Yes, of course, sir," Semenov said.

"Comrade Colonel Semenov, I need you to perform a most patriotic act. You are a patriot, are you not, Colonel?" Mikhailovich asked as he slapped Semenov on the back.

Semenov nodded uncertainly.

"Well, as you know, The Commander has tasked us with ensuring the Fascists do not capture this precious nuclear facility or our dam. It must not happen under any circumstances. It is too important. If it falls into their hands, why, they could use it to endanger our people back home or farther East. Do you understand, Colonel?" Mikhailovich said.

"Of course," Semenov said, while having next to no idea what Mikhailovich was on about.

Mikhailovich stood closely to Semenov. His intensity was

deeply unsettling.

"Colonel, I have been told of a wicked plot to deploy the materials inside this facility against the Motherland," the Lieutenant General exclaimed. "Can you imagine? They intend to use this awful material in our cities, Comrade Colonel! Against our women and children!"

Mikhailovich could sense Semenov's unease. Abruptly switching gears, he smiled before putting his right arm around the young officer's shoulders. "Colonel Semenov, I need you and a group of patriots to take an artillery battery and destroy the cooling stations at the nuclear plant and then blow the dam. Can you do that for the Motherland? Your nation needs you. Your Commander needs you."

Semenov was uncertain about these new orders. When they had attacked the plant in the early days of the Special Operation, it had been targeted and discrete. Though he knew it was risky, it was done to intimidate, not to genuinely destroy. Surely the purpose was to only hint at madness? To make the Nativists think they *might* do it? But to Semenov, Mikhailovich's eyes suggested otherwise. It was deeply unsettling.

"And the core? What of the core?" asked Semenov. "It might be hard to strike accurately in this environment."

"Well, accidents happen . . ." said Mikhailovich with a grin.

Semenov looked past Mikhailovich towards Golubev and Sokolov, desperate for some guidance from the other two officers. Golubev made eyes with the young soldier and subtly shook his head. It was all Semenov needed.

"I'm sorry, Comrade Lieutenant General. I can't. I, we, I – I must leave." And with that, he turned and walked briskly away from Mikhailovich. And then he ran.

Mikhailovich sighed. "Are there no patriots left in this pathetic outfit?" he spat.

He looked to the square where, despite the chaos, the Fascista was still performing her Nativist burial ritual. The very sight of her incensed him. Mikhailovich could feel the bile and blood rising in his body. Enough was enough.

With his left hand, Mikhailovich drew his pistol. "Well, seeing as though there are no real men left here, I shall settle this matter once and for all myself."

"A first time for everything," Sokolov muttered.

Mikhailovich ignored the comment. He was settled on his course of action and was determined to achieve his mission.

Sokolov and Golubev watched Mikhailovich walk slowly towards the square with his pistol by his left side.

Explosions were now hitting regularly and with force. The remaining soldiers were scattering to the vehicles. The convoy was leaving.

Sokolov stomped a half-smoked cigarette on the ground. It was time to bug out. He climbed into the rear of a nearby truck, now filled with soldiers and an incoherent scramble of equipment, supplies and looted booty. He looked at Golubev, who was still watching Mikhailovich making his long walk towards Oksana.

"Sasha, are you coming?" Sokolov asked.

Golubev ignored him.

"Sasha, we cannot wait. We must leave!"

Golubev was barely paying attention to anything Sokolov was saying now. Not even the nearby explosions or shocks of booming sound would break his gaze.

"You know who her father is?" Golubev said.

"What?" Sokolov asked. It was impossible to hear over the sounds of the looming war.

"I said, do you know who her father is?" Golubev yelled.

"Sasha, we do not have time for this game. They are coming!" Sokolov begged.

"Well, do you? Or do you only pretend?"

"Of course, I do! That is my job, to know. Now, get in the truck, Sasha – that's an order!"

"Would he have left her?" Golubev yelled.

"Sasha, there is no time. Do not do this now. It was different then. It was all different! The lines had not been drawn. Please, we must go!" Sokolov screamed, his hand outstretched to his friend.

Golubev took one last look at Oksana. "Good luck, Miss Shevchenko," he said, sighing deeply.

With a sense of shame, Golubev turned towards the truck.

But he had not moved in time to avoid the incoming

shell. The ensuing explosion to the right of the truck sent Golubev flying into the air.

As the truck roared away, Sokolov stared at the smoking crater behind him. Inside, he could see a bloodied Golubev, lying face down.

Sokolov watched silently as the crater and the city disappeared into the distance.

* * *

Oksana was holding the fourth and final flag in her hands.

Staring ahead, her eyes were fixed on the town's flagpole, located in the very centre of the city square. Atop it still flew the flag of the Motherland.

Oksana knew this flagpole could be seen in every direction approaching the city. Given that the flag could be seen by the approaching Homeland armies, she knew it had to be removed.

The Heroes had to know they had friends here.

"You will stop this instant, Miss Shevchenko!" Mikhailovich yelled from across Union Square with his gun pointed in her general direction.

Oksana ignored him. The explosions grew louder and closer again. She began walking towards the flagpole.

"Miss Shevchenko! Do not test me!" Mikhailovich yelled over the sound of sirens, gunfire and exploding artillery.

And then suddenly, the world grew quiet.

The explosions and the noise stopped. Nothing.

The guns firing both ways had fallen quiet.

Oksana could only hear the crunch of her boots on the ground. And Mikhailovich's.

She knew the silence was telling. The Heroes were proceeding unimpeded. They were coming.

With renewed determination, she vowed they would not return home to a false prophet flying in their square.

"Miss Shevchenko! You will stop right there!" Mikhailovich yelled. Seeing the silken colours in her hands, Mikhailovich realised what Oksana was up to. This was a final humiliation that he would not allow.

Oksana refused to listen, refused to turn.

Mikhailovich fired a warning shot into the air.

"One," Oksana said to herself instinctively. The sound of Mikhailovich's crunching boots quickened behind her. She did not turn back, but instead urged herself onward.

Two more shots rang out from Mikhailovich's pistol. These both passed over her head.

"Two, three," she whispered.

Gradually, the doors of homes and apartments surrounding the square opened.

The people had been watching from behind drawn curtains and hidden vantage points. They had been waiting. Patiently. Just as they had for hundreds of years, through various indignities and oppressions.

Their time was coming.

People draped in yellow and blue began to flow outside. At first a trickle. Then a torrent.

Mikhailovich heard them before he saw them. They were humming. Humming that awful music. How he hated that music.

Oksana began to repeat the poetry of her homeland to herself as she walked.

Even though she hadn't recited it well over a decade, the words came flooding to her and out of her yet again.

"And when the blood
of our nation's foes flows
into the blue waters of the sea,
that's when I'll forget
the fields and hills
and leave it all
and pray to God."

Another shot rang out. It whizzed past her head. And then another.

"Four, five," Oksana said before continuing with the poem.

"Until then, I know no God.
So bury me, rise up,
and break your chains.
Water your freedom
with the blood of oppressors."

Buoyed by the words, she began to pick up her pace.

"Miss Shevchenko, this is your final warning!" Mikhailovich screamed.

Oksana was now at the flagpole. Looking upwards, she began to turn the crank to lower the flag of the Motherland. Even though she knew Mikhailovich was near, she would not stop.

Watching that vile Nativist woman lower the flag of the Motherland from roughly fifty feet away, Mikhailovich steadied himself, aimed, and pulled the trigger.

Oksana felt a sharp sting in her left thigh. A few seconds later, another in her shoulder. She felt the warmth pouring from her wounds, but no waves of pain, not yet. She had to keep going.

"Six, seven," Oksana said before unclipping the Motherland's flag and attaching the flag of the Homeland.

Mikhailovich began running. He had to stop her. No matter what happened, it would not end this way for him.

Around Mikhailovich, the humming was getting louder.

"And then remember me
with gentle whispers
and kind words
in the great family
of the newly free."

Oksana slowly began to raise the flag upwards. She lifted her head as the blue and yellow silk rose into the sky.

And then she felt it. The barrel of a pistol resting on the back of her head.

Mikhailovich steadied. Oksana closed her eyes and breathed in deeply.

"For the Motherland," Mikhailovich said.

"For the Heroes," Oksana whispered, still looking upwards at the flag.

The eighth and final shot rang out. The rope fell from Oksana's hands.

It was the last thing she heard.

* * *

Oksana's body lay on the bed inside the small room.

A soldier stood watch over her, holding flowers, his head bowed.

Though youthful, his face wore deep lines of weariness. His army fatigues bore the colours of the Homeland. His eyes were red, exhausted from a night spent keeping watch. A night spent berating himself.

He had been too late. He had broken his promise to her.

If only he had gotten there sooner. If only he had hurried. Then these bastards wouldn't have hurt her.

A doctor entered the room.

"Have you slept, young man?" she asked, smiling at the soldier as she went about her business.

The soldier smiled sheepishly, sweeping the blonde hair from his face.

"Now, I know you soldiers are made of tough stuff. But even cyborgs need to rest," the doctor said, opening the file hanging next to Oksana's bed. She looked up at the young man. "She's going to be okay, Private Shevchenko," the doctor said reassuringly. She closed the chart and hung it back into its place.

Dmytro looked down at his sister, who was lying on the thin hospital bed, asleep.

"She just needs rest," the doctor said, patting him on the back. "Just like you."

Dmytro grinned. "Doctors orders, huh?" he said, looking up at her.

"Exactly. She is in good care, son. We will look after her. Now, go home!" She playfully pushed Dmytro towards the exit.

The soldier turned and began to walk out of the room. The doctor was right; he was utterly exhausted, and Oksana was safe. That, along with winning the War, was all that mattered.

"Dmytro?" said a quiet, strained voice from behind him.

He turned. She was awake.

Oksana couldn't believe it. "Dmytro . . ." she said, her eyes welling with tears as she recognised her brother rushing towards her. "How . . . ?"

But before she could say another word, the words poured from Dmytro's mouth as he ran to his sister's bedside. "One of the orcs from their side – an officer, actually, from the Motherland – he shot the Lieutenant General. At least that's what we think. It was impossible to tell, given they were both dead. A sort of solid older fella was lying next to you; he'd bled out. We're still trying to identify all of these bastards, even if they're gone to hell. Do you know him?"

Oksana's mouth hung open. "I . . . I don't know. I was pulling up the flag and . . ."

"Even though they were in retreat, there was so much confusion and chaos. I thought you were gone, sis. When I saw his body on top of you, and you had been shot. And the blood . . . well, I thought the worst." Dmytro was struggling to get the words out fast enough.

Suddenly, he stopped and looked at Oksana. "I thought I had lost you," he said, his eyes glistening with tears.

"Dmytro. Oh, Dmytro, it doesn't matter. It doesn't matter . . ." Oksana said, taking her brother's hand and placing it against her face. "You are home."

Through the window, Oksana saw the colours flying proudly across her city. The sun shone onto her face. She could smell the cherry blossoms in the breeze.

She smiled.

It was all glorious.

CHAPTER 28

Under a clear blue sky, the sun rose over a free land.

Against all odds, the people had prevailed.

A hope built over centuries of oppression.

A flame carried between generations.

A stolen history returned.

A freedom paid for in blood.

Once more, the black tide had been reversed.

The Reaper was returning to his crypt.

And in the East, The Commander sat nervously.

For He was all alone.

And soon it would be His turn.

A NOTE FROM THE AUTHOR

Why I wrote this book

To spend a week in Ukraine is to fall in love for a lifetime.

Her vibrant cultural heritage, physical beauty and complex history are all uniquely captivating and utterly spellbinding. But it is the Ukrainian people – who maintain a sense of humour and boundless optimism under unspeakable duress – who are the most magical of all.

With the future of democracy on the line, what happens in Ukraine matters everywhere.

The outcome of Russia's invasion of Ukraine will have an outsized impact on global affairs for decades to come. We cannot simply watch in horror. Our fates are intertwined.

A Note from the Author

* * *

"We in Ukraine are like a chicken bone that breaks," my server Anya, a woman in her thirties with two school-age children, tells me inside a small restaurant in central Kyiv. After some discussion in my average Russian and her superior English, we laughingly deduce she meant "wishbone". It's mid-February 2022, and Anya is worried what will happen to her kids if war breaks out, as seems to be likely.

I still think about Anya. I don't know where she is, but her words on the eve of conflict were prophetic.

Ukraine is the fulcrum in a broader battle between the East and West. Between democracy and autocracy. Between the future and the past.

The Sun will Rise is a story of ordinary people doing extraordinary things because the times demand it. It is dedicated to the brave people of Ukraine and their fight to be free from Russian tyranny.

Why Fiction?

When Russia's latest invasion of Ukraine began, the world hoped to dismiss it as a regional conflict that would soon become part of history. Instead, it has become a parable for a much deeper struggle for the future of humanity.

So much has already been written and said about these awful events that another contribution to the field risks being lost in the clutter of content. But the power of story conveys meaning in a way that dispassionate facts and figures simply cannot.

Stories and character act as conduits for essential truths while offering the reader a timelessness that is often lost in non-fictional diatribes. Story gets to the heart of a matter that academic analysis, for all its rigour, can sometimes miss.

We remember stories. We care about characters. They hold up a mirror to all of us. And that's why we we need them.

The Sun Will Rise is my small attempt to detail the horrors of what I have witnessed inside Ukraine and explain to you why you must be invested in Ukraine's success.

Growing up, I remember listening to the stories and struggles of World War II and the Cold War from my Deda and Babi. While undoubtedly horrible, it all felt sepia-toned. These were remote, historic struggles that could never be repeated in their brutality or ideological mindlessness.

And yet here we are. Again.

The Sun Will Rise might be a story inspired by Ukrainian bravery, but it is a reminder to the world about the price of freedom. Evil cannot be reasoned with; it must be defeated. Refusing to do so today only raises the costs of doing it tomorrow. The only question remaining is how long it takes us to remember – and act upon – this repeating reality and what damage is caused in the meantime.

I hope you can connect with the timeless truth of this

struggle. And if so, then please do everything you can to help defeat the bad guys. Their victory is for all of us – because there is no guarantee who will be in the firing line next.

Remember, absolutely everyone wants to be free. And together we can make the world a better place.

A Word on the Characters.

At the outbreak of war, I was struck by how many women leaders were at the forefront of the national effort. Whether it was Stacya, an eleven-year-old school girl who was donating her pocket money to the cause; or young politician Vikka, leading a refugee resettlement initiative; or Ivana, who cooked hot meals for cold volunteers as her seven of her grandsons fought on the front lines – at every level of the country, women were all rolling up their sleeves to take Putinism head on.

Though it was perhaps a coincidence, the centrality of women to Ukraine's defence was a striking juxtaposition to the failed machismo of Putinism, whose armies were floundering. In my experience, the Ukrainian Superwoman is real.

The heroes of *The Sun Will Rise* happen to be women. All are an amalgam of the people I met along the way inside Ukraine. But in truth, every Ukrainian is a hero.

The use of female protagonists was not a deliberate choice, but as I wrote the story, I drew on my experiences and memories of people I'd met throughout the country. And, like any writer will tell you, characters have a way of emerging in the mind's eye as though they exist in real life. For whatever reason, this felt right. And it felt true.

If you recognise yourself in any of the characters, know that you have inspired me. And if you don't, well then, consider that a failure of the writing!

A Word on the Use of History.

The Sun Will Rise is a fictional story based on true events that have occurred during Russia's invasion of Ukraine. To provide context to the actions of Vladimir Putin, the book draws on the complex history of Ukraine and its long, fraught relationship with Russia.

This makes *The Sun Will Rise* a "trueish" story of what has happened in the past and how we got here. It is a reminder to the world of the consequences of allowing darkness to grow unabated.

Keen eyes will recognise my use of recent and historic events. At times, I have renamed or recast certain facts to suit the narrative arc, but I have tried to remain loyal to their core and essential truths.

Where there are errors of historical fact or interpretation, they are my own. Where there have been deviations from accepted history or a condensation of characters and events, I have done so for literary expediency. Please accept these have been done with good faith and not in an attempt to recast matters of historic importance.

A specific note I wish to address: I have slightly edited the prose of Taras Shevchenko from his poem "My Testament". The edits were done for the purpose of context only and de-identifying specific uses of Ukrainian geography and names. I make this acknowledgement as it involves the borrowing of work that is not my own. Given the significance of Shevchenko to the Ukrainian independence struggle, I felt it was important to include his work within the body of the narrative.

For those interested about Ukraine and Russia, or who are eager to more fully understand the issues I have raised, I encourage you to read extensively. Other readers of this book have enjoyed deeper dives to learn about major issues or historical events that I can only point to within a short story.

The Ukrainian coat of arms features an image of a trident. The now-ubiquitous blue and gold flag has become a global symbol for freedom and democracy.

The Trident was the ancestral sign of the original rulers of ancient Ukraine, the Rurik dynasty (10th–12th century, Kyivan Rus). Archaeologists still find its image on coins, seals, utensils, bricks and murals. In the tenth century, coins bore the image of the Prince of Kyiv, Volodymyr the Great.

The ownership of this symbol and Russian claims to Ukraine's ancient history is one of the key motivations behind Vladimir Putin's invasion. The complex, nuanced history between Russia and Ukraine – who defines it and who acts as its righteous protector – is at the very heart of Putin's war, and Putinism more broadly.

For centuries Ukraine has been caught between its Western, liberal leanings and the eastern pull of Russian domination.

Putin's invasion has forced Ukrainians to choose once and for all. And we must stand with them.

ACKNOWLEDGMENTS

Any book is the product of more than just the author. And this is absolutely no different.

Firstly, I want to thank the Ukrainian people, whose spirit and personal generosity to me have made all of this possible. It has been the honour of my life to tell your stories of incredible bravery to the world. I know you will secure your freedom from tyranny, and I hope this story inspires the world to continue its support of this most vital cause.

To the many Ukrainians I have met along the way who have shared their homes, stories of heartbreak and hopes for the future with me: I want to thank you all from the very bottom of my heart. You have all given me far more than I can ever repay you in return.

I want to thank Editor-in-Chief of *The Australian*

Financial Review, Michael Stuchbury, for backing my journalistic endeavours inside Ukraine. Essentially, there are two ways to become a war correspondent. The first: spend twenty years learning the craft of journalism while grinding it out in a newsroom and earning the right for an international posting. The second: turn up in a war zone and commence corresponding. Stutch, I couldn't have done any of this without you. So thank you.

To the team at Forefront: thanks for backing an unknown Aussie taking a punt on a story he cares about.

To my editor, Amy Kerr: thank you for your generosity of insight. Your help in smoothing the sharp edges of my writing has been wonderful and improved the final product immeasurably.

To my mum, Jackie, who read various iterations of my draft manuscript enough times to qualify as a form of torture: a big thank you.

And to the love of my life: thank you for being you and giving me the confidence to put this idea out into the world. I hope my squawking about the manuscript wasn't too tedious. You're an incredible woman who inspires me to be better.

ABOUT THE AUTHOR

Misha Zelinsky is a leading authority on the rise of authoritarianism.

A Fulbright Scholar, economist, lawyer and author, Misha has extensively covered Russia's invasion from inside Ukraine as a war correspondent for *The Australian Financial Review*. He is personally sanctioned by the Putin regime.

A Master's graduate from the London School of Economics and Political Science, he is an expert associate at Australia's National Security College and a director of AustralianSuper, a superannuation pension fund with over $300 billion under management.

Thanks to his time as a leader of the Australian Workers' Union – Australia's oldest blue-collar trade union – Misha has been a leading political figure with a reputation for expertise in supply chain sovereignty, national security, industrial policy, countering foreign interference, international trade, and energy security.

As a contributor to MSNBC, BBC and ABC, Misha's work features in Australian and international print publications including *The Australian Financial Review*, *The Sydney Morning Herald*, *The Daily Telegraph*, *Foreign Policy Magazine*, and *The Times of London*. His 5,000-word profile from inside President Volodymyr Zelensky's hometown won wide acclaim.

Misha is a regular columnist *for The Australian Financial Review* and *Foreign Policy Magzine*, writing on the future of democracy, Australian domestic policy, national security and geopolitics. He is the host of the popular foreign policy podcast *Diplomates – A Geopolitical Chinwag.*

Misha's family is Russian-Ukrainian in background and he is Russian-speaking. His family fled from Soviet oppression in the 1940s and currently resides in Australia.